MURDER STORY

MURDER STORY

John Wainwright

Chivers Press • G.K. Hall & Co.
Bath, Avon, England   Thorndike, Maine USA

MAY   9 1995

This Large Print edition is published by Chivers Press, England, and by G.K. Hall & Co., USA.

Published in 1995 in the U.K. by arrangement with Little, Brown & Company (UK) Ltd.

Published in 1995 in the U.S. by arrangement with Little, Brown & Company.
U.K. Hardcover   ISBN   0–7451–2990–0   (Chivers Large Print)
U.K. Softcover   ISBN   0–7451–2997–8   (Camden Large Print)
U.S. Softcover   ISBN   0–7838–1143–8   (Nightingale Collection Edition)

The text of this Large Print edition is unabridged.
Other aspects of the book may vary from the original edition.

Set in 16 pt. New Times Roman.

Printed in Great Britain on acid-free paper.

British Library Cataloguing in Publication Data available

Library of Congress Cataloging-in-Publication Data

Wainwright, John William, 1921–
  Murder story / John Wainwright.
    p.   cm.
  ISBN 0–7838–1143–8 (lg. print : sc)
  1. Large type books.   I. Title.
[PR6073.A354M87   1995]
823'.914—dc20   94–33674

MURDER STORY

PART ONE

THE FAT MAN—THE BUSY-looking man—said, 'It's our bread and butter, you know. We can't afford to have produce systematically stolen, like this. I think it's one of our employees, but I can't be sure. And, I don't want to accuse anybody without—'

'We'll see to it. We'll see to it. The tone was brusque and dismissive. The speaker was a copper. Very much a copper. He looked like a copper. His name was Cullpepper; Detective Sergeant Owen Cullpepper.

The entrance hall of Rogate-on-Sands Police Station was unduly busy. Uniformed and plain clothes officers, of both sexes, were bustling around with that look of strained expectation on their faces which is a by-product of having been caught on the hop. The fat man had almost had to elbow his way to the public counter, and now he was cross, because nobody seemed to be taking much notice of him.

He'd buttonholed Cullpepper as that officer had been passing the counter, on his way to the CID offices, on the first floor. Cullpepper, who'd been up little more than an hour, was already starting to feel the strain of unusual responsibility.

The fat man said, 'North of England Pork Products. We're not a small firm, but we can't—'

3

'In a *minute!*' interrupted Cullpepper, angrily. 'Dammit, man, the jewellers in Main Street were ram-raided in the early hours of this morning. A few thousand quid. That's what we're dealing with. Not a bit o' bacon.'

'Look, I don't see why—'

'We'll get to you, we'll *get* to you,' snapped Cullpepper. 'Just don't get under our feet. We have *real* crime to see to for the moment.'

A slim man, slightly shorter than the average police officer, entered the police station. He had quiet authority, and the others parted to give him space to cross the entrance hall and open the door marked 'Private', which led into the various sanctums of the building.

Cullpepper turned to a uniformed constable and, *sotto voce*, said, 'Get rid of this clown. The boss has just arrived. He'll want the details.'

Cullpepper, in turn, hurried towards the door marked 'Private' and disappeared from the entrance hall of Rogate-on-Sands Police Station.

The fat man had not caught Cullpepper's words, but he'd certainly realised their purport.

He dismissed the uniformed constable before that officer could speak, and said, 'Oh, forget it. There must be a *better* way of getting things done than this.'

Dodging his way through the slight press of coppers he left the police station in a huff.

                    *   *   *

Two hundred miles south of Rogate-on-Sands, it was cold in the capital. Christmas was a recent memory; recollections of the office parties were not now sufficient to warm the heart cockles, and the secretary birds scuttled for the central-heated comfort of their various cubby-holes as the north-westerly whistled down Edgware Road. The Young-And-Upwardly-Mobile types dodged into various wine bars and brasseries, to beat the chill, while the Old-And-Downwardly-Slipping shoved their hands deeper into the pockets of their coats and silently cursed the bloody weather.

Two men turned right, into Sussex Gardens. One was tall, and immaculately dressed. The other was merely well dressed, middle-aged and with a fixed but pleasant enough smile on his face. They walked in step, without undue haste and as men who knew each other well. They turned left, into Southwick Street, then left again, into a cul-de-sac which preceded the Cambridge Square turn-off.

At the end of the cul-de-sac, the house was a typical, good class, detached property; well-maintained and standing in its own area of neatly kept garden ... but, it wasn't. It was, in fact, one of the most select private clubs in the whole of London. At any given time, it was the location of the biggest game in town—craps or poker. Roulette was on the first floor, chemmy was on the second, and the one-armed bandits were in the basement. Wagers were any size the punter fancied, from a few quid to something likely to make an oil sheik's eyes pop.

The top floor was fitted out as a luxury flat; the home of the guy responsible for the quietly smooth running of the place. It never closed and, given time, could cater for anything—legal or illegal—the man footing the bill had in mind. But always with fitted-carpet-and-bevelled-mirror style; without fuss, without noise and without come-back.

The two men climbed the shallow steps to the door of this establishment, pressed the bell-push and were admitted. They rode a lift up to the top floor, left their outer clothes in the entrance hall of the flat, then strolled through to enter a small, but immaculately furnished room off the main lounge. Beautifully framed, soft-porn photographs punctuated the expensively decorated walls. Quality coffee-tables were strategically placed alongside deep and inviting armchairs, and two other men were lounging, in obvious comfort, in two of those chairs. One of these men was white, with a severely crew-cut hair of vivid ginger, the other was deep coffee-coloured, with the features of an angry hawk, and shoulder-length, jet-black hair.

They rose to their feet as the two newcomers entered the room.

Ginger-head said, 'Taske? Ed Taske?' The

three words which made up the double question pin-pointed his place of origin. New York ... not a hundred miles from the Bowery.

The tall newcomer gave a quick, old-fashioned nod of the head, and said, 'That's me. Edward Taske. This is my colleague, Edward Manser.'

'Hi.' Ginger-head's face split into a welcoming grin, and he stretched out an open hand. 'Lew Fame—Red Fame to my buddies.' They shook hands, and Fame added, 'This is Tom Boy Collins. Full-blooded Pawnee. A warning, mac. Tom Boy can tell when a man's lying. And he's never wrong.'

'Really?' Taske raised an eyebrow, turned to lower himself into an armchair, and drawled, 'I have a similar ability. Manser, here, merely kills those I *find* to be lying. It saves a lot of wasted time.'

Fame's eyes flipped from Taske's face to the already seated Manser. The .38 calibre Llama automatic pistol was held in a gentle but steady grip. It rested on Manser's knee and was obviously in the hands of an expert.

'Hey, mac,' protested Fame, 'this is no way to start negotiations.'

'We are not here to negotiate,' said Taske, from the softness of the armchair. 'My brother, Henry, concluded all negotiations, with your boss, in New York, more than a month ago.'

'Things change.' Fame returned to his chair, but kept an eye on the Llama.

7

'The deal is either on or off. That is the only change—the only option—left open.'

'Hey, mac—'

'Not "mac",' said Taske. 'I've never worn a kilt in my life, and I detest the sound of bagpipes. My name is Taske—that or "sir".'

'You short a few ball-bearings, mac?' Fame's tone hardened.

'On or of?' snapped Taske.

'If you can handle the distribution.' Fame's friendliness had evaporated.

'If you can handle the delivery,' countered Taske.

'Hey, mac,' snarled Fame, 'I tell the men up top about this reception—and don't think I don't.'

'The "men up top",' murmured Taske, 'won't mind if I send you back without balls, just as long as the money's good.'

The Llama kept Fame pinned to the chair. It also kept the American Indian very still. Without the Llama things might have been a little different.

Taske said, 'Your side are responsible for getting the first kilos as far as the Irish coast. Then we take over.'

'Off the Irish coast, mac. *Off* the Irish coast.'

'Quite. We'll get it *onto* the Irish coast ... Once it's there.'

'Two weeks from today, mac. You'd better *be* there. If not, the Haslop outfit are ready.'

'Ready for what?' Taske's tone was as gentle

8

as a feather dripping cyanide. 'Ready for street warfare? Ready to be blown away? Tell me, Fame, is this talk your own personal brand of garbage? Or are you carrying messages from those who sent you?'

'Just so you know you're being given top-grade merchandise, Taske. The sort of stuff the boys on the street are screaming for. Just so you know that.'

Taske rapped, 'I'm being "given" *nothing*, little man. I'm paying top price for top stuff. Any more stupidity from goons like you and the deal's off—and you can pass that message to those who sent you.' Taske pushed himself to his feet and added, 'Two weeks from today, Fame. At the agreed co-ordinates. At noon. Make sure your people are there—or don't bother to come.'

The man called Tom Boy had been easing his right hand, slowly, towards his left armpit. The fingers touched the haft of a bowie knife, and the shot from the Llama sounded like a miniature cannon in the enclosed space. The American Indian gave a quick yell, and jerked as the shot took him in the right shoulder, but, despite the obvious pain, the fingers still tried to curl themselves around the knife's handle. A second shot smashed the silence of the room, and the hand dropped as its owner quietly sobbed with pain.

Taske said, 'Have a quiet, man-to-man talk with your partner, Fame. Advise him not to be

9

too heroic—it could kill him.'

*   *   *

In his cups, and sometimes out of them, Harry Thompson would call himself a 'private investigator'. In effect, it meant that he swept up the nail parings of those inconvenient little incidents which were not quite criminal offences, not yet important enough to be covered by the Law of Tort. He smoothed out rough surfaces. He delivered quasi-official ultimatums. He grubbed around trying to find enough evidence to prevent a case—*any* case— being laughed out of court.

He 'knew people'. Years ago he'd been an almost successful investigative journalist on a second-rate tabloid. He'd figured himself a cross between Bernstein and Woodward ... but that had been undiluted kidology. Instead of immortality, his nasty little investigations had resulted in the threat of libel actions and, eventually, the mother-and-father of nervous breakdowns.

Thanks to his wife, plus a removal-van-sized load of tranquillisers, put-to-sleepers and quietener-downers, he hauled himself back to some degree of sanity, and his long-suffering wife had succumbed to his plea to stop short of an all-out divorce and, instead, had been satisfied to separate from him.

By this time, of course, Thompson was

something of a character in the tiny seaside town. 'Thompson of Rogate-on-Sands' was the general Man Friday who collected all the problems too minor for the coppers, and not important enough to merit a solicitor's fee. His office-cum-living-quarters above *The Wine Bibber* was known to the various do-goodery organisations—official and unofficial—and the advice 'I should have a word with Thompson' was, by this time, the general let-out when all reasonably sensible suggestions had had no result.

He had many acquaintances but few friends. The coppers of Rogate counted him as a necessary pain in the neck. His wife tolerated him, but secretly wished he'd move out of her life, and give her the freedom to find another mate, without a feeling of massive guilt. Bull Adams, the owner of *The Wine Bibber*—and also Thompson's landlord, tended to treat him as an errant son; excusing, advising and occasionally, criticising—but never with the severity required to have any effect.

This, then, Harry Thompson: a pygmy who thought he was a giant, a weakling who figured himself to be Atlas.

He had a hangover, which wasn't too unusual on a Monday morning. He soaked in the tiny bath, which was in the tiny bathroom, which was part of his tiny living quarters, above *The Wine Bibber*. The 'book of words'—by which he meant any American

11

private eye novel—insisted that the finest cure for a hangover was a needle shower. Scalding hot, followed by icy cold. But Thompson didn't have a shower and, had he had one, wasn't too crazy about cold showers, needle or otherwise. He therefore soaked in the warm water of the bath, enjoying make-belief relief from his troubles via the thick, creamy foam and the almost overpowering smell given off by the Christmas present of a bottle of green-coloured glorified washing-up liquid.

The telephone bell rang.

Thompson muttered, 'Sod it!' and made no move to leave the bath.

The telephone continued to ring and, eventually, with ill grace and trailing carpet-soaking wetness in his wake, Thompson heaved himself from the bath, left the bathroom, crossed the hall and padded his wet way into the living-room.

He lifted the receiver from its wall rest and grunted, 'Thompson Detective Bureau'.

The caller said, 'May I speak with Mr Thompson, please.'

'Speaking.'

'Ah, Mr Thompson. My name's Eagan. Managing Director of North of England Pork Products.'

'Good morning, Mr Eagan.'

'We'd like to employ your firm, on a matter of theft, Mr Thompson. Are you available?'

'We can certainly discuss the matter, but I'm

12

very much tied up at the moment,' lied Thompson.

'As soon as possible, please.'

'Tell me, Mr Eagan, have you been to the police? If it's theft, I mean.'

'It's certainly theft, and I have been to the police. But they don't seem too interested.'

'Why is that, Mr Eagan? Did they tell you?'

'Something about a jewel robbery. Bacon don't interest them.'

'Really?'

'So, when can we expect you, Mr Thompson?'

'Later today? This afternoon, perhaps?'

'I'll be here, in my office. Three-thirty, perhaps?'

'I'll certainly try to get there.' Thompson figured being hard to get could justify an extra nought on the final bill. So he repeated, 'I'll try to get there, Mr Eagan. If I can't get there, I'll certainly ring and let you know.'

He replaced the receiver and, shivering from the unexpected exposure to the draughts of the flat, hurried back to the bathroom and warm towels.

As he dressed, he pushed the telephone conversation around in his head and decided that the unknown 'Mr Eagan' was of the Jewish race. The way he'd said 'don't' rather than 'doesn't' gave the first clue ... but, hell, Jews and Pork Products didn't go together. Or maybe they did. Thompson knew it to be a big

13

firm, and to sell the stuff didn't give a warranty that they *ate* it.

It was (Thompson decided) a lousy, mixed-up, and very hypocritical world.

* * *

Taske had moved south of the river. Just a fleeting visit—a quick, in-and-out job—because south of the river, and especially Wandsworth, was strictly Haslop territory. Taske would have denied being scared—indeed, he was *not* scared—but simple prudence had decreed that the visit be mob-handed, and with iron. Taske and five of his hardest 'soldiers' made the taxi seem overcrowded but, no matter, having crossed Wandsworth Bridge they turned right, rolled along High Street, then turned right again into one of the dozens of narrow streets poking back towards the Thames.

The taxi braked to a halt outside a greasy-spoon cafe, and the men inside the taxi moved with swift, military precision. Two jumped out of the vehicle, raced a few yards left and right, then stood in a half-crouch, right hands at their left armpits, guarding the approach to the taxi from both up and down the street.

Two more men left the taxi and positioned themselves as shields—again, both left and right—as Taske left the vehicle, followed by Manser. Manser already had his Llama

14

unholstered, and was ready for trouble.

Taske ducked into the cafe, followed by Manser and two of the gunmen. The look-outs moved back, towards the cafe, and stationed themselves at each side of the door, on the pavement, their backs against the wall.

The cafe was empty except for one customer, the proprietor and the scruffy guy who served at the counter and tidied away the dirty crockery.

As Taske and Manser entered, the proprietor snapped, 'In the back, boy,' and the scruffy guy looked scared and scuttled out of the body of the cafe and into the private quarters at the back.

Taske said, 'Excellent advice. Now follow it yourself.'

'Eh?' The cafe proprietor stared.

Manser pointed the Llama and said, 'Make space, friend. We're still one too many, and you're it.'

The proprietor looked as if he would have liked to argue, but he changed his mind and followed the scruffy guy into the back.

The customer smiled his appreciation.

He was an Asian gentleman, flamboyantly dressed in fur-collared overcoat and a dark green, wide-brimmed trilby. He rested gloved hands on the not-too-clean table-top and murmured, 'You are remarkably punctual, Mr Taske.'

He smiled a very enigmatic smile as Taske

15

joined him at the table, and said, 'I hope this dangerous meeting will be worth while.'

'You,' said Taske, without preamble, 'are one of those wise birds who sometimes sell twists of Harpic as cocaine. That is what I am told.'

'Those who tell tales are not always to be believed.'

'It shows initiative. The Harpic trick, I mean.'

'It does no harm. Less harm than the real stuff.'

'And if you could *get* the real stuff?' said Taske.

'Ah, yes.' The Asian gentleman smiled his enigmatic smile again. 'Then I would not have to purchase Harpic.'

'You have discos, night-clubs, dance halls.'

'That is my business. Quite legitimate, I assure you.'

'Of course ... discos, night-clubs and dance halls.'

The Asian gentleman hesitated, then said, 'You have snow for sale?'

'Snow?' Taske's deadpan expression went with the quasi-innocent question.

'Nose candy. Coke. The sniffing stuff. It has many names.'

'Cocaine?'

'You seem unwilling to commit yourself, Mr Taske. May I put it bluntly, please? Yes, I talk of cocaine. Of crack. Of amphetamines ...

speed, uppers, bennies, ecstasy. Of drugs which addicts foolishly seek, and which I can often supply. If not from me, from some other person. Why should I deny *myself* certain luxuries?'

'Why, indeed?'

'They are doubly foolish. They know what they are doing. They have been warned—for years they have been warned ... but they still seek their stupid pleasures. Why should *I* deny myself?'

'Quite. And you have an easy outlet.'

'Many outlets, Mr Taske. Many friends, who also have outlets.'

'I do not deal with "friends" nor "friends of friends". Only with you.'

'Understood.'

'We should have a dealing place. Outside London.'

'Manchester? Nottingham? Bristol? I have places of entertainment in most of the big cities.'

'Manchester.'

'Manchester it is.' The Asian gentleman nodded, then added, 'The small matter of money, Mr Taske? May we?'

'My brother, Henry, will be in touch. He deals with the more sordid side of things. Just that you *can* spread the commodity to the community—that is what *I* have to ensure. That *I* can get it, and that *you* can dispense it.'

'Rest assured, Mr Taske. I am to be trusted.'

'As with all our business associates,' said Taske gently. 'You are to be trusted, or you are to be buried.'

One of the men from outside poked his head through the door and said, 'Trouble, boss.'

Without any real hurry Taske rose to his feet, grasped the Asian gentleman by the upper arm and steered him towards the door of the cafe.

From the street came the snap of three quick shots, followed by the sound of a motor vehicle crashing. As Taske, Manser and the Asian gentleman left the cafe, the taxi had its engine running, the two outside guards were standing with guns drawn, and the two gunmen from the cafe had joined them, their own weapons trained onto an ancient Rover whose front nearside tyre was in shreds, and whose bonnet was crumpled against a lamp standard. From the Rover, large men were tumbling out onto the street. Five of them. Five men, two pickaxe handles, a machete, a police truncheon and a length of lead piping. Manser sent a round ricocheting off the road surface and the opposition dived for shelter behind the Rover.

Taske bundled the Asian gentleman into the taxi and climbed in himself, followed by Manser and the four bodyguards. Then the taxi drove off, back into High Street, back across Wandsworth Bridge and back into the safe territory of Fulham and Hammersmith.

It had been a mere nothing. A few moments

18

of explosive violence in which two gang lords had, figuratively speaking, touched gloves. But no more than that. The greasy spoon cafe would suffer fairly extensive damage, as, indeed, would its proprietor. But that was par for the course and only to be expected. It was the way the Taske gang and the Haslop gang exchanged pleasantries.

* * *

The man looked exactly what he was; a hard-nosed, middle-ranking cop. The barrel chest, the slabs of muscle, the heavy jowls and the fixed scowl gave him away. He was part of 'The Sweeney'—the Metropolitan Police Flying Squad—and, as such, expected lesser men to tremble in trepidation whenever he showed even mild displeasure.

The scruffy guy who served at the counter of the greasy spoon cafe was reporting the morning's incident to his superior.

He said, 'It was Taske, guv. Taske and Manser. And some of the heavies from the Taske Force. But I don't know the coffee-coloured goon.'

'Dope?' The one-word question was growled from the back of the throat.

'Everything. From aspirins up.'

'It follows. The Yankee narcotics crowd pass the same grif.'

The scruffy guy looked, and sounded,

19

disappointed as he said, 'I couldn't do much else, guv. Not without blowing my cover.'

'You did right, kid. Just get back there and clock the Haslop turds. *We'll* deal with Taske and his army.' Then, as an afterthought, 'What happens to Joe, the cafe owner?'

'They've already broken his arms.' The scruffy guy put in very little expression; it was part of normal, everyday retribution, broken arms. He added, 'I reckon his wife takes over till he gets upright again.'

'And the cafe?'

'New windows. New crockery. A couple of new chairs and a table.'

'They let him off lightly.'

'Yeah. They could have torched the place. That's what I expected.'

'Y'see, son.' The older cop looked pensive. 'We don't *really* have to police the bastards. Just let 'em get at each other's throats. That's all. Haslop's mob went easy because they know that if they get *too* carried away, Taske's mob will tear one of *their* places down. Checks and balances, see? A sort of equilibrium. One day some smart-arse is going to work it all out, scientifically, and reduce it to a formula. Then,' he grinned, 'we shall all be able to go home and draw our pension.'

*   *   *

The pillar-box red Porsche nosed its way off

20

the M1, turned right and moved with the other traffic, west along the North Circular. The driver figured it to be the most uninteresting— the most monumentally boring—stretch of road in the United Kingdom. Neasden. Harlesden. North Acton. Ealing Broadway. They sounded like tiny, rural communities; rustic villages complete with pond, pub and green. But they weren't. They were merely one barely identifiable part of the sprawl. Before the Clean Air Act, winters there had been deadly—*literally* deadly. Now the brickwork and stonework still carried the marks and scars of innumerable smogs and pea-soupers. Pseudo-modern jostled with Victorian and mock-Georgian rubbed shoulders with would-be avant-gardism. The result was a hodge-podge of dreary, uninteresting houses, shops and offices, with nothing along the whole stretch of the North Circular likely to catch the attention of any passing motorist.

The woman knew the Porsche, and knew the road. She drove with the smooth, natural skill of somebody who has spent a lifetime behind the wheel of expensive motor cars. She was mid- to late-forties, very well preserved and very expensively dressed.

She was a whore—and, like most top-line whores, she didn't *look* like a whore. She'd been in the call-girl racket when she was in her twenties, had chosen the punters with care, given good service for expensive sessions and, at her best, had been scooped up by the Taske gang who'd been out to clamp a monopoly on the north-of-the-river prostitution set-up. Eddie Taske had fallen for her and married her, and, for a while, she'd tried respectability for size. Her natural instincts had however got the better of her, and she'd gone back to happy fornication as a means of countering boredom.

And here's a thing...

The criminal fraternity mirror-images the police service, in that both worlds have their own jungle telegraph. A big shake-up in the force, and every copper from Devon and Cornwall to the Highland Region has wind of it before it takes place. A massive theft to be committed, and the big-time villains get the smell before it happens. Nobody specifically *tells*, but, like water through cloth, the information seeps its way through, and both those who should, and those who shouldn't, get to know.

Thus the woman knew about her husband's coming involvement with the import and the distribution of drugs. Not 'when', not 'how' and not 'who', but enough information to make her worry.

She knew about drugs. If necessary, she could tell some very hairy tales about her sisters-of-the-sheets, who had sniffed, swallowed or injected various nasty substances in the pious hope that the result would be a gentler, less violent life-style. She knew the error of such ways, but she also knew that there was nothing she could do to dissuade those hell-bent on self-destruction.

She kept on the North Circular until the junction with Chiswick High Road, then she turned left, and on, along King Street and into Fulham.

* * *

It was a nice office. Not too large. Not too small. Nice and cosy, with a moderately sized desk, a desk chair, a bank of filing drawers, a selection of easy-to-sit-upon chairs, some pleasant wall prints and a fitted carpet. Very nice, but it was part of a building which handled dead pigs, therefore there was this vague, disgusting smell.

Thompson figured it was something nobody could shift. Like the antiseptic pong of every hospital in the world. It went with the job.

Thompson had correctly figured Eagen to be a Jew. He said, 'We ain't gonna have no thieves working here.' And that was the give-away. The natural use of the double negative. He added, 'Trouble is, we don't know which ... see? We want to be *sure*.'

'If it's theft,' said Thompson, 'you should go to the police. It's what they're paid for.'

'We ain't going to no police,' said Eagan flatly. 'If it ain't jewels, they're not interested. Lemme tell you, Mr Thompson. Bacon costs

23

money. Sixty-two pounds, cash, for a side weighing seventy pounds, weight. That ain't cheap. Fifty-eight pounds, cash, for a sixty-five poundside. I don't touch the stuff—well, not *much*—but the Gentiles like it, and I'm in business. Some schmut is robbing me blind, and the police ain't interested. That's why you're here.'

'I'm not cheap,' fenced Thompson.

'So, who's arguing?'

'Forty quid a day.'

'That way we save money.'

'Or, per part of a day.'

'Why not?'

'Plus expenses.'

'Naturally.'

'Mr Eagan.' Thompson's tone had a hint of desperation. 'I tell you the truth. I don't like taking over from the official cops. *They* might not like it. That could make things very awkward for me.'

'No way.' Eagan shook his head. 'My lawyer tells me it's okay, if you hand the evidence over to the police. That's what we want. Nothing private. Nothing underneath. Everything up top and plain printed.'

'It's just that—'

'If not you, somebody else,' said Eagan. 'I open the Yellow Pages. They're there. Lemme tell you. All my life I pay for the health service, but I don't *use* the health service. I don't want no part of it. I pay. That way, *I* tell the medic what to do, and when to come. The same with this. I pay for the cops, but I want my own man, working for *me*. You see that?'

'I'll do my best,' promised Thompson. 'Just that I don't want you to get wrong ideas. I don't cover things up. Theft—if it *is* theft—and I tell the cops, without even asking for your go-ahead.'

*   *   *

Edward George Arthur Adams—more commonly known as 'Bull'—was a product of Her Majesty's Armed Forces. Smart as paint, ramrod stiff and with a step and a bearing that belied his fifty-plus years, he'd left the army, invested his savings in a run-down cafe off the front at Rogate-on-Sands, gutted it and created *The Wine Bibber*. A combined wine-bar, eating house and tiny, intimate boozer. He'd chased away all undesirables, and threatened to tear the head off anybody who even threatened to put a wobble on his own, private apple cart. And prospered.

Go into any British Legion club and you will see 'Bull' Adams, cloned up to a dozen times. Ex-NCO. A continual worshipper at the shrine of discipline and, in particular, self-discipline. Glaring of eye. Slightly florid of complexion. The one-time terror of recruits, but a man of simple principles and a man who once upon a time would have been described as a typical 'yeoman'.

Originally the idea had been for him to retire to Rogate, run the establishment, and live in the upstairs rooms while, when he wasn't busy, he could keep a fatherly eye on his daughter and her husband, and a grandfatherly eye on her twins. Something hadn't been quite right in the set-up. For perfection all round it had been necessary for him to live *with* his daughter and her family. The rooms above *The Wine Bibber* had become empty, and Harry Thompson had jumped at the chance of making the upper rooms into the 'Thompson Detective Bureau'.

And that was the reason for the present altercation between Bull Adams and Detective Sergeant Owen Cullpepper.

'Not,' said Cullpepper importantly, 'a dwelling house.'

'They lived here before,' argued Adams.

'Eh? Who?'

'The horrible types who ran it before I came here. They lived in the upstairs rooms. I was going to do the same.'

'It was *theirs*,' growled Cullpepper. 'A cafe thing, with living quarters as part of it. You sub-let.'

'There's nothing in the lease,' said Adams.

'Ultra vires,' said Cullpepper pompously.

Adams muttered, 'I didn't know.'

They were sharing a table in the eating half of *The Wine Bibber*. They each had a part-consumed cup of coffee. In truth, Cullpepper

26

was laying it on even thicker than usual, but Adams had the old soldier's fear of illegalities he didn't understand, and tended to be a little intimidated.

'While I'm here,' said Cullpepper off-handedly. 'A niece of mine. Getting married in a couple of months. Thereabouts. I was thinking about your place for the reception.' He added, after a pause, 'If it's reasonable, that is.'

'We don't do receptions,' said Adams.

'As a favour, eh?' Again, a very meaningful pause. 'One favour for another. That's what I mean.'

'We don't do receptions,' repeated Adams. Then, in a tone tinged with anger, 'And we don't do *anything* on the cheap.'

'I thought I'd ask,' said Cullpepper.

'You've asked. The answer is that we can't accommodate.'

'About Thompson,' murmured Cullpepper, mildly.

'Harry stays.' Adams glared a little. He said, 'I don't know. You may be right. You may be wrong. Either way, I don't think it's a police matter. When whoever deals with these things gets in touch I'll see what I have to do. Meanwhile, finish your coffee, Sergeant. It's on the house. Then, if you don't mind, I have work to do.'

*   *   *

27

The red Porsche nosed its way from the main thoroughfare and into the almost hidden Fulham off-street. It turned off the carriageway, and the up-and-over doors of the garage opened automatically, as the car broke the electronic beam.

The driver of the Porsche was too concerned with her own thoughts to take much notice of the mini cab which had followed her from the busier road. Nor, when she left the garage and made for the large, detached house, did she notice the two men who left the mini cab and angled their way towards her.

She became aware of danger only when the razor-sharp blade of the knife slipped through her clothes and bit into the flesh of her side.

From behind her the man's bent arm clamped around her neck, and he said, 'No screaming, no struggling—nothing, or else it goes in, haft deep.'

She tried to nod, but couldn't, from the pressure of the bent arm.

As they climbed the steps to the porch, the closed circuit TV camera swivelled on its overhead pivot and kept its single eye pointing down at them.

There was a grilled loud-speaker by the door, and from it came an electronic likeness of Taske's voice.

'You're being very foolish, whoever you are.'

The man with the knife said, 'Maybe, but

this blade goes in, deep enough to kill, unless we're inside before anything else is said. And clear passage to whichever room you're using.'

The knife-man's companion began to look scared. His eyes jerked from right to left as he watched for approaching danger.

Five slow and deliberate seconds ticked their way to eternity. The silence was complete enough for them to hear the purr and hoot of the traffic on the hidden main thoroughfare. Then the silence was snapped by the click of an electronic bolt leaving its housing.

Taske's voice said, 'The door's unlocked.'

The knife-man tightened his grip on the girl slightly, then said, 'Lead the way, lady. You'll know which room. But don't forget to behave yourself.'

She pushed open the unlocked door and they entered the house. Awkwardly the two of them crabbed their way through the hall and along a short passage. She pushed open a door with her foot, and they entered a large, airy room whose high windows looked out onto the side garden.

As the door to the room was pushed open, the knifeman's companion lost his nerve and, with a soft, strangled squeal, ducked down by the wall of the passage, then scurried for the still open door.

He gasped, 'I'll—I'll have the car waiting.'

The knife-man's concentration didn't waver. He entered the room with the woman's body directly in line between himself and its

29

two occupants. He kicked the door fully open before he spoke.

Then he said, 'Haslop wants a meet.'

'Haslop does?' Taske's voice was as quietly controlled as ever. There was the hint of a smile brushing his lips as he spoke.

'He has the connections. He could help the distribution.'

'*Haslop* could?'

This time, Taske *did* smile. Manser, too, smiled. Taske was standing with his back to a large, ornate fireplace, in which burned a gas-fuelled fire which gave the impression of almost half a hundredweight of coal blazing away up the chimney. Manser was seated in an armchair. Manser had his Llama nestling in his lap; it looked quite ordinary, and not at all lethal; as if Manser habitually relaxed in a deep armchair with a automatic pistol cradled in the fold of his thigh.

The knife-man said, 'Haslop says to tell you. Brighton, Hastings, Folkstone. All the way to Bournemouth and Poole. He has the outlets.'

'You're here to tell me that?' Taske seemed to be genuinely amused.

The woman whispered, 'For Christ's sake, Eddie. This bastard has a knife at my ribs.'

Casually—in a deliberate, throw-away tone, Taske said, 'Shoot him Manser. Through *her*, if necessary.'

The woman gave a quick, high-pitched squeal. Manser raised the Llama from his leg.

The knife-man had the simple gumption to realise that Taske wasn't even *trying* to bluff; that Manser was about to send a bullet into him whether or not the bullet passed through the woman first.

The knife-man released the woman and tried for a backward dive, into the passage, beyond the open door. Manser squeezed a shot off and hit the knife-man in the leg, just below the knee. The knife-man howled in pain and rolled on the floor of the passage. The woman almost collapsed when the knife-man released his grip, steadied herself, then ran from the room and for the front door. The knife-man rolled in the passage and sobbed with pain. Taske strolled towards him and, quite deliberately, stamped his heel onto the wound, beneath the knee.

Taske murmured, 'The world is full of idiots. They think they can get away with *anything*.'

The knife-man screamed, once, then fainted.

Manser joined Taske in the passage, tilted the gun, and said, 'Do I blow him away?'

'No.' Taske glanced at the unconscious figure and said, 'Find a sack. Parcel him up, label it "Returned to Sender". Then hire a cab and deliver it to the goons across the river.'

*   *   *

The wind howled up from Avonmouth and hit Bristol like an iced shower. It raced east and along the river, then seemed to gather strength as it battered the environs of Temple Meads Station.

Harry Thompson watched his quarry from the small shelter given by vehicles in the car park. He popped a few more shots off, and hoped the film in the camera was fast enough to show some detail in the shadow. Not that it mattered too much. The pictures he'd taken less than an hour back in Mangotsfield showed enough detail for a certain conviction, and all the creep wanted now was to feed his face in the railway buffet, before shooting back north, along the motorway network.

Thompson toyed with the idea of himself catching a snack at the buffet, before he, too, drove back up north. He dismissed the passing notion as a shade too risky. The van driver was a stranger but, presumably, he lived in or close by Rogate-on-Sands. This meant that he just *might* recognise a fellow inhabitant of that borough, and it was asking the gods of coincidence to be rather over-active in getting two burghers of that fair but tiny borough to meet up in a railway station buffet a couple of hundred miles from home. And in this weather, too.

The weather was gradually but definitely worsening. The temperature was brass-monkey orientated, the wind wasn't easing at all and snow showers of blizzard proportions were forecast.

Thompson shivered, and remembered all the

Yankee private-eye novels he'd read. Not a word about skulking around in freezing cold, photographing bacon stealers. The fictional gumshoes always ended up handling sophisticated murder in a warm climate. They were rarely beyond reach of some nubile, eager female and never without the comforting weight of lethal ironmongery in one or more pockets.

Whereas, in the United Kingdom...

He sighed, figured he'd earned his fee for the day. He pocketed the camera and ducked between the parked vehicles, to where he'd left his own car.

*   *   *

Taske was on the telephone. He spoke quietly enough, but the words had an unaccustomed bite.

'Sure. She's taken the damn Porsche, which means she's some sort of destination in mind ... Okay, but I want her stopped. Followed, if necessary, but stopped ... If necessary ... Yes. Permanently, if necessary ... Sure. I'll fix all the alibis necessary. Just take her out of circulation ... That, or bring her back here and I'll handle things ... Let me know when, okay? And don't horse things up too much—right?'

*   *   *

'Luck,' said Lyle wisely. 'Better than fingerprints. Better than all the test tubes and scientific ga-ga. A touch of luck, and detection is as easy as falling off a log.'

Detective Sergeant Cullpepper sniffed, and pretended to look interested.

'If,' continued Lyle, 'those ram-raiders hadn't been amateurs—if they'd had the simple gumption to try a respectable fence when they offered the stuff for sale—'

'If they hadn't been scouse dumb-bells,' grunted Cullpepper.

'—we might never have recovered the stuff.'

'Have we?' asked Cullpepper.

'From what the Liverpool boys say. It was offered as a job lot, and the jeweller it was offered to played along, then informed the police.'

They were in Lyle's office; a modest but very modern room within the structure of Rogate-on-Sands Divisional headquarters. It was an airy room, but warm enough, thanks to an efficient central heating system. Pastel shades predominated, with two framed rectangles of modern art positioned neatly on the wall space. The desk, filing cabinet and glass-fronted book case boasted that plain, no-nonsense simplicity which screamed 'expense', and the chairs were all matching tubular and leather works of genuine craftsmanship.

It was some office, and Lyle loathed the place.

It was late evening, and after a moderately busy day both officers were ready to drive home, eat, then sprawl in front of a warm fire until bed-time.

Their Liverpool colleagues had just telephoned good news and, truth to tell, Lyle couldn't quite understand why Cullpepper wasn't more enthusiastic about the outcome of the recent ram-raid.

Cullpepper said, 'I wouldn't mind policing Liverpool. Something of a doddle, really. Everybody oak-thick. What more can you ask for?'

'Don't let me stand in your way,' said Lyle.

'Eh?'

'But, take heed, Sergeant. It's uncommonly hot in that particular kitchen.'

An expression of dislike touched Cullpepper's expression for a moment, then he said, 'I hear your friend Thompson has a job that should be ours.'

'Thompson?' Lyle raised quizzical eyebrows.

'The town's tame private dick. I'm told he's chasing bacon somewhere.'

'I hope he knows what he's doing.'

'He'll feel safe—being a friend of yours.'

'Easy, Sergeant,' warned Lyle. 'If he oversteps the mark, he's in trouble. And he knows it. You, too, would be wise to give some thought to that possibility.'

'I didn't mean—'

'Yes, you *did*. But that's as far as you're going.'

Cullpepper compressed his lips, but remained silent.

Lyle stood up from the desk chair and said, 'That's my stint for today. If you've nothing else to do—'

'I haven't.'

'I thought not. Away home, Sergeant. Get your feet up.'

Cullpepper moved to leave the office. As he reached the door, Lyle spoke again, this time in a quiet, almost apologetic tone.

'Sergeant.'

'Sir?' Cullpepper paused and waited.

'I wouldn't want to deceive you, Sergeant. In case you haven't yet tumbled. I don't particularly like you.'

'Oh!'

'I don't like the way you police. All this bish-bash-wallop stuff leaves me unimpressed.'

'I see.' Cullpepper's voice was quite deadpan.

The words, 'In fairness, you should know,' rode what amounted to a soft sigh. 'You have very little leeway, as far as I'm concerned. That's what I'm saying.'

'Nice to know.'

'Not "nice". Cautionary, perhaps, but not "nice".'

'Quite so.'

36

'Away home, Sergeant. Now we both know where we stand.'

* * *

North of Bristol, Harry Thompson moved from the M4 to the M5. It was dark, it was cold and he had a three-figure drive ahead of him. Most of it was going to be motorway driving, with oncoming headlights and the glare in the rear-view mirror of more headlights from vehicles about to overtake.

It was going to be a long, weary drive, and the business of private detection could result in very nasty, very tiresome, situations.

He sighed, changed the tilt of the driving seat a little and settled down to some long, long miles of boredom.

PART TWO

The man being murdered didn't know he was being murdered.

At first it was a push between the shoulder blades. Then it felt as if somebody had kicked him in the back; high up and slightly to the left. He staggered forward and had a surprised awareness that he was unable to correct his balance; that he couldn't bring his own gun to bear. His last thought was that he might stumble and tear a hole in the knee of his trousers on the crushed ash underfoot.

He was dead before he hit the ground.

*　　*　　*

It was about fifteen minutes into a new day, and I'd driven too far without a break. I'd parked in a quiet corner and was toying with the idea of catnapping before treating myself to tea and a bite prior to tackling the last fifty miles or so.

I had that warm, satisfied feeling of a job well done. Way back, in the outskirts of Bristol, the refrigeration van had unloaded two sides of cured bacon, the buyer had paid the driver a fistful of notes, and I'd snapped off half-a-dozen telescopic-lens shots.

As always, Lady Luck's eyes had been twinkling in my direction. 'As always', because that sweetheart's approval is *always* necessary.

41

I'd picked the right day. The tailing job, down the motorway, hadn't been too difficult. The positioning of my own car, at the scene of the switch, had been comparatively easy. Nothing had screwed things up and the evidence was in the camera case, on the back seat.

I yawned, looked at the dial of the radio and decided not to switch the set on. Some of the crap they push out may keep weary drivers awake but, for me, the non-interest might have cancelled everything out and made for added irritation.

I glanced around the car park. If you've seen one Service Area you've seen them all. The spill of light from the main entrance seemed to emphasise the gloom and shadows where the light couldn't reach. The park was about a quarter full but, somehow, that only made it look a lot more than three-quarters empty. Away to my left beyond the flower-bed dividing line—the six-, eight- and ten-wheelers were parked in the lorry park.

Once upon a time all tarpaulins had been black. Now they were all the colours of the rainbow, complete with tailored shapes and stitched roping.

No matter. Tarted up or not these monsters were kings of the road, and the men who drove them deserved all the luxuries of a secure load and a modern cab. Night-driving, even on decent wheels, is no push-over. Handling one of those brutes, with oncoming headlights hitting your face, has to be the sort of job only masochists enjoy.

It switched my wandering attention back to the main entrance of the restaurant block.

A yellow AA van pulled up to one side of the shallow steps. A uniformed driver climbed out and ran up to the glass doors. For the o'clock he had a lot of spring in his step, and I envied him. I also wished he'd trip and fall on his fanny. When he reached the top he held the door open for a neatly dressed female to greet the nip of the night air.

She was alone and didn't seem to be one little bit worried by that fact. Maybe she didn't read newspaper reports about lone ladies being raped on motorways.

She, too, was more awake than was decent. The lights above the entrance were like floodlights. They magnified and made more obvious the first flakes of falling snow. They gave her a background glow that bordered upon the ethereal. Maybe that was why I watched her with more than usual interest.

She was wearing a light-brown overcoat against the January weather; a belted overcoat with a wide, high collar. Her hat was of the same colour and, like the cuffs of the coat, it was fur-trimmed. The calf-length boots were a rich brown and they had that dull sheen only good leather can claim.

Away to the left—at about ten o'clock—a

43

car engine kicked into life.

I didn't look. I was too busy watching the woman.

I heard the rev of the engine and the climb up the gears faster than normal. First—second—third—then the woman turned her head. She realised before I did. She started running a whisker of time before I tumbled to what was happening. What was *going* to happen.

Then I, too, saw the car and had no doubts.

She could run. She ran like a man; legs pumping and knees high. She leaned her body forward, kept her elbows tight and her mouth open to gulp in the night air. She raced for the parked vehicles as the car reached the corner of the park and tried for a skidding turn.

She, too, had Lady Luck with her.

The temperature had dropped dramatically in the hour or so before midnight. The steady drizzle of the late evening and early night had frozen here and there and now the snow was covering patches of thin ice which spotted the car park. The controlled skid wasn't controlled for long.

The rear end swung much too far to the left and, before it could be corrected, it smashed into the back of a Ford and the bonnet of a Honda. Nor did it do much for its own boot and rear mudguard. It also made a lot of noise.

The woman dived for the gap alongside my own car, mis-timed things and sprawled.

The AA man reappeared at the door of the

main building. An elderly couple joined him from inside. But it was too late. The car, crippled though it was, raced for the exit from the Service Area and the comparative safety of the dark motorway.

*   *   *

I said, 'My name is Thompson. Harry Thompson.

'Mason. Kay Mason.'

I gave a little nod at the rear-view mirror and said, 'Nice to meet you, Kay Mason. A mite unexpected, but nice.'

A few moments earlier, as she'd sprawled alongside the car, I'd leaned back in my seat and opened the rear door. She'd scrambled in and ducked down, behind the front seats. The interior light hadn't been on more than a couple of seconds and, when the AA man hurried up, I was sure he hadn't noticed it. I doubt if he noticed *me* until I'd wound down the window and leaned out to block his view of the inside of the car as much as possible.

I'd called out, 'What the hell was *that* all about?'

'Did you see it?' The AA man had looked outraged.

'Drunk?'

'Was he?'

'I don't know. He came from over there.' I'd waved a vague hand.

45

'Oh.'

'Like a bat out of hell,' I'd amplified.

'Did you get his number?'

'No.' I'd tried to sound mildly disappointed, then I'd added, 'Did you?'

'No.' The AA man had looked very sad, and added, 'Dammit. I'll have to get back inside and trace the owners of these other two cars.'

'Sooner you than me.'

'Yeah.'

He'd turned and walked back towards the entrance steps and, when he was half-way up the steps, her face had appeared in the mirror, and she'd introduced herself.

She said, 'I'm afraid I seem to have broken something in my hand. When I went down, I think.'

'You want me to check?'

'No. No lights—please.'

We stared at each other's reflections for a moment. I pulled an ear lobe, and began, 'Is there any good reason why—'

'There is no good reason.' She'd reached the end of my sentence before I had. She went on, 'No good reason at all why you shouldn't send me on my way.'

'That's what I thought.'

'On the other hand, why start things and not finish them?'

'I could have told the man you were here.'

'Agreed.'

'I could have told him what I'd seen.'

'Which wasn't much.'

'Why *shouldn't* I, even now?'

We looked at each other through the mirror. She was only a face in deep shadow. Hardly distinguishable in the back of the car. But she was there and she had a distinct 'presence'.

She said, 'Had I not injured my hand, I would wish you good night and return to my own car.'

'End of encounter,' I murmured.

'The decision is yours, Mr Thompson.'

'And for the rest of my life...'

'Yes?'

'I'd wonder.'

She ignored the remark, and said, 'I *could* drive.'

'In that case—'

'But motorway driving—at night—with a broken hand. It wouldn't be very sensible.'

'The last few minutes,' I countered. 'Whatever else, they haven't been "sensible".'

'No,' she agreed.

'Whoever was in that car—'

'Two men.'

'They seemed to be out to kill you.'

'That was the object of the exercise.'

'In that case—'

'*Had* they killed me it wouldn't have mattered. To them, I mean. Unfortunately— fortunately for me—things went wrong. They attracted attention.'

'And now?' I asked.

'They have a job to do.' She was remarkably calm. 'They won't rest until they've done it. Or until they've been called off—or, perhaps, frightened off.'

'The police?' I suggested.

'Some Constable Plod?' Her tone carried smiling contempt.

I said, 'Some policemen tend to know how many beans make five.'

'Really.'

'Don't let TV cops give you wrong ideas.'

'No police,' she said firmly.

It was a crazy conversation but not for a moment did I doubt her seriousness. If there was the hint of tremor in her voice, who could blame her? She'd almost been rubber-stamped into the tarmac. Had it been me, *I'd* have had a tremor in *my* voice. Maybe I *had* a tremor in my voice, and it *hadn't* happened to me!

I fell back on the old stand-by. I fished cigarettes and a lighter from the glove compartment and lighted a cigarette. I tried to think things over, but couldn't. I hadn't enough facts to make sense.

I had a moderately well-dressed, moderately well-spoken, moderately attractive woman on my hands. She'd been moderately injured and was being moderately brave about it. After that, moderation went down the tube. After that, everything was left-hand threaded.

I blew out my cheeks and puffed smoke through pouted lips.

'I think we should move,' I said. 'The mad car enthusiasts might be back. They might try again.'

'Not tonight.' She sounded very sure and I hoped, for her sake, she was right. She went on, 'But I agree. We should move. Otherwise the AA man might get round to asking silly questions.'

'Silly?'

'Inconvenient.'

'Ah!'

'Awkward,' she decided upon.

I turned the key, gunned the engine, slipped the stick into first and eased the car towards the park exit. I kept the lights off until we were on the slip-road.

I said, 'North, of course. But where?'

'Junction thirty-three. Then on to Glasson. To a village about five miles west of Glasson.'

'Where's Glasson?'

'Just south of Lancaster.'

We were on the M6—leaving the Service Area south of junction twelve. Junction thirty-three was way and gone to hell up north.

I growled, 'My junction was going to be thirty-one.'

'That was before you decided to play knight-errant,' she returned.

I glanced in the mirror. I could just see her teeth bared in a smile. They were nice teeth and the smile was very friendly.

I said, 'Yeah,' and concentrated on driving.

49

The truth is, I did not *want* to be too friendly. Not to this one. I had a worrying gut feeling that I was being carefully positioned for some form of patsy treatment. When the time was ripe, of course.

It was not a very nice feeling.

*   *   *

Some people claim to enjoy motorway driving. Some equally crazy people claim to enjoy night driving.

The first crowd argues that motorways take you from A to B with the minimum of hassle; no roundabouts; no traffic lights; no unreasonable speed limits. The other crowd argues that the small hours see fewer vehicles on the road; fewer hold-ups; less chance of a shunt; a greater sense of being in control.

The complete goofballs claim that the best driving of all is night driving on a motorway.

Great—if your idea of a good time is travelling through a tunnel at breakneck speed with a stroboscope flashing in your eyes!

For my money, motorway driving at night is one of the least pleasant of a whole list of modern tortures. The road noise, the engine noise and the wind noise combine to assault the ears. Very gently, but without let-up. The steady, threatening whoosh of one more juggernaut creeping up past your right shoulder and, very gradually, overtaking—

giving the frightening impression of some legendary monster quietly moving in to pounce and swallow you whole.

And the lights. Those damn lights! Coming towards you. Bouncing back from the rear-view mirror. Controlled by lunatics who refuse to dip. Handled by long-distance men who 'talk' to each other with their headlights. The orange indicators, flashing and dying, and sometimes not being cancelled by some driver whose attention has wandered.

I blew out my cheeks and said, 'We learn the hard way.'

'I beg your pardon?'

'This puts the better part of a hundred miles on my journey.'

'I'm sorry.'

The first letter of the second word had an emphasised hissing quality and the rest of the word was snapped off in a rising hiccuping gasp.

'Pain?' I asked.

'I think something's badly broken. In my left hand.'

'I'm sorry.'

'It's not your fault. It's not—'

'I mean because I don't carry First Aid.'

And, having told each other how sorry we both were, we stopped talking for about five miles.

That, too, was okay by me. I am no great conversationalist. Nor do I like my attention diverted when I am easing down on an accelerator and trying to coax a few more miles an hour, within the strict limits of moderate safety.

The small hours—the ugly, ungodly hours—were easing into the time frame. My sleep rhythm was becoming too interrupted for comfort. I should not have been driving a motor car along a motorway. I should have been asleep and dreaming about much pleasanter things.

She said, 'I've thought of a better way.'

'Congratulations.'

'There's a Service Area a few miles south of junction thirty-three.'

'So?'

Drop me there. I'll phone home. If my husband hasn't got back, I'll take a taxi.'

'Your husband?'

'He's been at a Farmer's Union conference. He was going to try to get home last night. Late. If not, first thing this morning.'

I grunted and kept my eyes fixed on the road.

'You sound surprised.' I had the impression that she wanted to talk. 'Surprised that I'm married, perhaps?'

'You don't look like a farmer's wife,' I parried.

'Not plump and rosy-cheeked? Is that what you mean?'

'I'd say an air of *savoir-vivre*.'

'I'm flattered.'

'I fancy it's been mentioned before.'

'Not by a complete stranger.'

'Lady,' I reminded her, 'this "complete stranger" just might have saved your life. On the face of it, it's possible.'

'Much more than "possible".' If there had been a tendency to banter a little it disappeared. 'A certainty, in fact.'

'Why?'

'*Why?*' She made believe not to understand.

'Why should anybody want to kill you?'

'Mr Thompson, be advised—don't press for an answer.'

That was when the feeling came, like the rush of boiling milk up the inside of a pan. I didn't want the responsibility of having saved her life. It was a stupid and impossible wish; a wish to turn back time, like pressing the zero button on a stop-watch, to a point where the AA man held the doors open for her. Then what? What would I have done? What *should* I have done?

I said, 'You know who they were, of course?'

'Of course.'

'But, of *course*.' I gave a tiny nod at the rear lights of the high-loader I was following. 'Very few people drive around deliberately trying to kill strangers.'

She didn't answer.

'You expect them to try again?' I asked gently.

'That is more than likely.'

'The police *should* be told.'

I heard the whisper of a noise from behind me. It sounded like a very gentle, very ladylike chuckle.

'Have I pulled a funny?' I asked coldly.

'Not deliberately.' Then, in a tone that held a teasing quality, 'Here's one for you. What if they *are* the police?'

'Running you down?' I mocked. 'Playing on-the-spot executioner, without the formality of a trial? I'm not too crazy about the boys with buttons, but I credit them with better things than that.'

'They can't help,' she said, and this time the words weren't a tease.

We drove in silence along another stretch of motorway. I wanted to think, and she seemed to have outlived the previous urge to talk.

What I'd done back at the Service Area had been pure, spur-of-the-moment stuff and not like me at all. I am not that sort of a guy. I am nobody's champion. Ladies in distress can *stay* in distress as far as I am concerned. I fix things—my job is fixing things—but only for money. Without the moolah things stay *un*fixed.

Thus, my personal creed.

At last I muttered, 'I have a feeling. A bad feeling. A very sour feeling.'

'Don't,' she said.

'I have a feeling I've let myself in for trouble.'

'No.'

'Lady.' It was more of a grimace than a smile. 'I have had lots of practice. I am an expert. I can smell trouble hours before it arrives.'

'Not this time, Mr Thompson.'

'You—*personally*—are trouble. That is what is coming across. You. And you already *have* arrived.'

'You've helped me, Mr Thompson.'

'Ah!'

'You won't regret helping me.'

'So,' I growled. 'First question. Just who the hell *have* I helped? To know that might clear the way for a little less worry.'

'I've already told you.'

'Mason?'

'Kay Mason.'

'And what, exactly, does this mysterious "Kay Mason" do for a living?'

'North of England rep for a multi-national. Also overseas buyer for a large British chain store.'

'Two very fancy-sounding jobs.'

'I suppose so, on the face of it.'

'Neither of which involves being run down by nasty men in motor cars.'

'You asked a question.'

'That I did.'

'I've given you an answer.'

'Have you? If so, not the complete answer.'

'The only answer I *can* give, I'm afraid.'

I decided not to press things. It wasn't

important. We were playing conversational footsie, and we both knew it. In fairness, she hadn't pushed the kidology too far and I made-believe I half-believed her.

I switched topics and asked, 'How's the hand?'

'Swelling and damn painful.'

'Uh-huh.'

'There's not much doubt. It's badly broken.'

'They might have something at the Service Area.'

'Aspirins, perhaps. It might kill some of the pain.'

'Sit back. Don't talk. We'll be there soon.'

*   *   *

A motorway Service Area restaurant at around 2.am on a cold and frosty January morning. That says it all. My mouth felt as if I'd been chewing algae. My eyes seemed to be bedded in broken glass. Every bone, fibre and nerve seemed to have its own private and exquisite ache.

In the restaurant area a group of long-distance men were huddled over a corner table playing a dreary game of cards while whatever it was they'd eaten had time to digest. They effed and blinded quietly, and without anger, not caring that their talk reached out into the empty room and could be heard quite distinctly by both the woman and myself. I didn't mind. Nor, it seemed, did she.

I shivered slightly; the somebody-walking-over-your-grave brand of shiver, as icicles seemed to brush my spine.

'Tea or coffee?' I asked.

'Coffee. Black.'

'Something to eat? Biscuits? A sandwich? A scone?'

'Nothing to eat, thank you.'

I guided her to a seat next to a radiator and, as gently as possible, helped her rest the injured hand on the formica top of the table. It was broken, all right. The metacarpal bones. At least one. Maybe more than one. The swelling had already ballooned the hand into a deformity and the wedding band was almost hidden in the puffed flesh of the finger.

In the foyer, when I'd examined the hand before entering the eating hall, I'd said, 'You need a hospital.'

She'd shaken her head. 'No. I'll—'

'Lady, that hand needs—'

'I'll get home, then send for my own doctor. He won't ask questions. A quick drink, then we'll bind it. Then I'll telephone home.'

I wasn't too worried. It was her hand. Her pain. Her decision. So we'd walked into the hall where they served the food.

I told myself I didn't give a damn. I was no charger-mounted knight. Not even a donkey. No lance, no sword, no nothing. Just a damn-fool curiosity that sometimes—as now—

tended to lead me astray.

I threaded my way between the tables, to the counter, and waited until a female with a rat-tails hair-do noticed me. I told her my companion had had an accident—that she'd probably broken a bone in her hand—and asked for bandage and a packet of aspirin. The aspirins were for sale, but the female had to raid the kitchen's First Aid box for a roll of bandage. I ordered tea and coffee, then went back to the table and sat down opposite the Mason woman.

I said, 'Right. First we play "doctors and nurses".'

'If you say so.'

The pain from the hand seemed to have subdued her. It had driven the colour from her cheeks and had narrowed her eyes.

'We need a fist,' I said.

'A what?'

'A fist.'

Cylindrical salt and pepper containers were on each table. I took one and held it out.

I said, 'Grab that. Wrap your fingers round it as tight as the pain will allow. Then I'll bind it.'

She did as I suggested. She even used her good hand to bend the fingers of her left hand around the container. Then I used the bandage to tighten and hold the fist in position.

It hurt a lot. It brought a few hisses of pain from her as I worked. But it was necessary if she was to be saved complications later. Without cotton wool it wasn't perfect, but it would do the trick until she reached a medic.

She released a long, slow and slightly tremulous gasp of breath and said, 'Thanks.'

I took cigarettes and a lighter from my pocket and when we'd both enjoyed that first, deep inhalation I motioned towards the cups.

I said, 'Coffee, before we do anything else. Then you can use the telephone.'

She sipped the coffee, drew on the cigarette, then stood up from the table.

She said, 'I'll telephone first. They can be on their way while we drink and wait.'

I didn't argue. Neither suggestion carried top priority. I nodded and, as she walked away, I stirred more sugar into my tea and enjoyed the cigarette.

Fifteen minutes later I finished the tea and stubbed out what was left of the cigarette. I was still alone. I wasn't too worried. She could have had trouble raising somebody at the end of a telephone wire at that hour. She could have slipped off to the john. Anything. I lighted a second cigarette and, when I'd smoked that and was still alone I grew suspicious.

I wasn't worried. I wasn't upset. Merely suspicious and vaguely annoyed.

I walked around the Service Area complex—the various foyers, the car park—but couldn't find her. All I found was snow and there was a little too much of that. It was starting to blanket and, in the strengthening wind, to drift.

I reached the conclusion that, in addition to being a tight-lipped and stupid cow, she was also an ungrateful cow. I drew what comfort I could by reminding myself that she wasn't unique. She wasn't the only ungrateful cow in the world. I'd met others. She was merely one more to add to my personal collection.

I muttered, 'And up you, Mrs Kay Mason. I hope *you* get played for a complete sucker one day.

I made my way to my car, left the Service Area, drove to junction thirty-three, then hammered south as fast as safety would allow. Towards home. Towards bed.

*   *   *

Home, let it be understood, is no palace. Nor is 'bed' an expensive four-poster.

Home is a pokey, self-contained flat behind my office, and both are above a wine-bar-come-eatery called *The Wine Bibber*. Bed is what the catalogue described as a 'studio divan', but comfortable enough as long as I have no burning desire to share it.

Both are inland from the promenade of a slightly toffee-nosed seaside resort on the west coast.

Rogate-on-Sands is no kiss-me-quick-and-roll-me-over holiday spot. It is a place of retired gentle folk, retirement homes, middle range hotels and enough trees, verges and flower beds to merit the description 'leafy' in its slim and slightly poverty-stricken brochure. It has no swings. It has no roundabouts. It has no whelk stalls. These attractions are available up the coast and down the coast, but at Rogate you get fresh breeze from the Irish Sea and, out of season, you get a deserted prom along which to stroll and stretch your legs.

At around four o'clock in the morning you get nothing.

The streets were deserted and, because I was too tired to make the effort, I didn't garage the car. I left it parked in the street by *The Wine Bibber*. I also glanced at the brass plate which read 'Thompson Detective Bureau' and, not for the first time, felt a twinge of embarrassment.

I was the 'bureau'. I was it and all there was of it. Not even a secretary. Not even a waiting room set aside from the office-cum-interview-room. And my qualifications for being a private eye added up to a few years of hot-shot investigative journalism, the very slammer of a nervous breakdown and a bust marriage.

I hadn't yet jumped on the corns of the local constabulary but, given time, that would come. Real coppers do not like clowns like me, and who can blame them? From the first, I'd given a firm elbow to any keyhole capers. I was no divorce-chaser, and that limited my work to criminal and near-criminal activity.

Like, for example, the whizz-kid I'd just photographed selling sides of bacon that weren't his to sell. I also had a running contract with a handful of hotels up and down the coast; to play 'customer' and check that the staff hadn't become too greedy.

I made enough loot to live on, but I was never going to be rich.

Not rich, then. But not poor. With a bed waiting for me to flop into. And my own man for twenty-four hours in every day.

It was with such high and philosophical thoughts that I closed the door, climbed the stairs and switched on the electric fire in the bedsit. As I undressed I found time to fill the kettle, switch it on and spoon instant coffee into a beaker. I rescued a slice of cold chicken from the fridge and buttered a couple of rounds of sliced bread.

The kettle boiled as I was showering, and having towelled myself into a glow I made myself coffee and a chicken sandwich before I slipped under the duvet.

This was luxury and to add sweet music to my joy I fed a cassette into the deck alongside the divan. Goodman came through with his signature tune, *Let's Dance*, and all the mysterious crap about strange women having motor cars aimed at them dropped into proper perspective.

I was a lucky man. I appreciated big band

swing and I lived where recordings of that brand of music could be played, whatever the hour. I had no neighbours. In the whole street, mine was the only address with living quarters.

As always, I marvelled. There was a smoothness, a professionalism and a determination in the Goodman arrangement, on a par with...

I couldn't duck it!

Despite the music, I couldn't switch off the memory.

On a par (if you like) with two unknown, homicidal bastards who'd driven the car at the Mason woman. It, too, had been deliberate. It had been cold-blooded. And there'd been two of them. One bearded. One clean shaven.

I frowned as the memory became fractionally less hazy. Once again I saw that moment of murderous malevolence. Two men. A dark coloured car. A dark *blue* car. Correction ... *maybe* a dark blue car. Just that the wash of light from the entrance had made it *look* like a dark blue car.

A Nissan. Suddenly, I was quite sure—a Nissan. A dark blue Nissan. Registered number? QV. But QV what? The scene came back, but through a mist. After the QV there was nothing. Nor was there anything *before* the QV. Just QV because QV was a crazy number. A crazy part of a registration number.

The Goodman orchestra bounced *Let's Dance* to a neat and tidy ending, then James (or

63

maybe it was Elman) blew a deceptively slow opening to *Bugle Call Rag*.

I finished the coffee and the chicken sandwich, put the beaker and the plate on the carpet by the divan, reached out and turned off the electric fire, flicked the lazy switch and allowed Goodman, Krupa, Griffin, Ballard and all the rest of them swing me all the way to Dreamland, with no hint of Nissans, no motorway Service Areas and no crazy women setting out to get themselves killed.

Only music.

*   *   *

I slept late. It was moving towards midday when I yawned the last of the sleep from my system, had a morning shower, shaved and dressed. I was due to make a call at the local police station to break the news about the misappropriation of sides of bacon, but first I needed food.

I did what I usually did on these occasions. I went down to *The Wine Bibber* and ordered what other customers called 'early lunch' and what I called 'late breakfast'; grilled bacon and kidneys with scrambled egg, followed by toast and lemon marmalade.

One of the few buddies I allowed myself— 'Bull' Adams, proprietor of *The Wine Bibber* and also my landlord—joined me at the table.

'When we closed shop at midnight, you

weren't home,' he accused.

'I was a long way from home.' As I ate I told him about the Service Area incident and the Mason woman.

'West of where?' he asked.

'Glasson. That's where she was making for.'

'That's wrong.'

'A village—maybe a farm—west of Glasson.'

'I know the district.' Bull scowled and added, 'Well, I know *Glasson*. Anwhere *west* of Glasson and you're in Morecambe Bay.'

I was brought up to believe that it was bad manners to speak with your mouth full. It was one reason why I chewed and waited.

Bull said, 'I have a pal lives at Glasson. A fishing pal. We sometimes fish from the mouth of the Lune. You take it from me, Harry. There's *nowhere* west of Glasson until you reach the Isle of Man.'

'Who cares?' I spread marmalade on toast.

'Sure. But why give you a dummy address?'

'Again, who cares?'

'I mean—if she thought you were going to take her home—'

'She did. I was.'

'Not to somewhere "west of Glasson", you weren't.'

'Okay.' I bit into the toast. 'Forget it, Bull. It's no longer important. Next time—whoever it is—they end up a nasty smear on the tarmac.'

'You don't mean that.'

65

'No? Don't bet your last pair of socks on it, friend.'

Things like that—remarks like that—tended to upset Bull. A one-time sergeant major in the regular army, he had a loud voice but a soft heart. He'd retired from khaki, bought a run-down cafe, turned it into *The Wine Bibber* and settled down to live with his daughter, her husband and twins at Rogate-on-Sands. When I set up shop as a private eye, he'd offered me rooms above the wine-bar-cum restaurant when my own marriage folded. I owed him a lot. I liked him. I liked him enough to rib him a little, and he liked me enough to take the ribbing.

'You,' he said, 'are nothing like the hard nut you make yourself out to be.'

'I'm a sissy,' I agreed. 'That's why I miss great chunks of sleep to help maidens in distress.'

I finished the meal, strolled through the town and ended up at the police station. I asked for Lyle and had no difficulty in being shown to his office. I dropped the folder containing a copy of my report to the firm paying me, plus photographs, onto his desk.

I said, 'The Case of the Demon Bacon Slicer.'

'Eh?'

Lyle was a cop. He was a detective superintendent. He had no sense of humour.

I said, 'A character helping himself to parts

66

of pigs that aren't his.'

'Oh!'

'It starts in this area, then goes way and gone to hell to all points of the compass. That's why the firm asked *me* to nose around before inviting you people to take over.'

He opened the folder and read the contents. He examined the photographs. He took his time. The impression was that he was seeking faults. He didn't find any.'

He murmured, 'Near Bristol?'

'Last night,' I agreed. 'Witnessed and photographed on three other occasions. Oldham, Chester and Wrexham. There's enough there to nail him. At a guess, he'll sing every aria in the book.'

'Why?' he sighed.

'Why what?'

'Why pay people like you? Why don't they just come to *us*?'

'You have to be joking.'

'It's what we're here for. We can—'

'You're gummed up with protocol.' I was telling him something he already knew, but didn't like being reminded of. 'You can't cross boundaries without saying "please" and getting permission.'

'Letting our colleagues know. That's all.'

'Wasting time.'

'Simple politeness.'

'"Requesting",' I insisted. 'And the guy you're chasing just *goes*. He doesn't have to

67

ask. Doesn't have to notify *anybody*.'

He grunted, then said, 'I suppose I should thank you.'

'Don't strain anything. Just don't object too strongly to the witness expenses.'

'Shall we need you?'

'Unless you want the photographs thrown out.'

'Uh-huh. I suppose.' He sighed. Then, 'Don't come *too* strong with the expenses.'

'I know,' I mocked, 'I have a civic duty to do *my* policing at cut-price rate.'

'Something like that.'

'Nothing like that, Superintendent. Nothing at all like that.'

*   *   *

Lyle did not love me, but that was a situation never likely to get between me and my sleep. Coppers do not love private investigators. They have their reasons.

If a copper bends the law all hell tends to pop. If a shamus bends the law he can horse around a little and, if he comes badly unstuck, he can play dumb; with a moderate amount of luck he only ends up with a swift smack in the teeth, and everybody feels satisfied.

Nor, thank God, is a private eye ever expected to tool around with riot shields!

I was not, therefore, too worried about Lyle's considered opinion. Especially so when the bacon curers greeted me with smiles and kisses. I was (the managing director assured me) the best investment they'd ever made. I would (he further assured me) be called in if so much as a pig's squeal ever went missing in the future. With that, he accepted my bill, signed a cheque and, with smiles all round, it was a world of warmth and happiness.

Not outside it wasn't.

Outside it was classic January weather. Cold, with more than a feathering of snow in the angles where the salted breeze couldn't work its melting magic.

I decided to give myself a break for the rest of the day. I strolled to the end of the pier, watched a handful of enthusiasts freeze to death while they fished for dabs then, when the cold began to drive in too deeply, I returned to the town and enjoyed an early dinner at one of the better hotels.

I stayed there until almost nine o'clock then, hoisting my collar against the strengthening breeze, zig-zagged through the streets and into *The Wine Bibber*.

At the bar I ordered a dry cider and, as the barman was pouring it, Bull strolled up and murmured, 'Cullpepper's been in. He's looking for you.'

I collected my drink and walked to a table. Bull accompanied me.

I said, 'I am not Cullpepper's favourite person.'

'That I know.'

'Did he mention why he wants to see me?'

'No.'

'It can't be important then. I'll call in and see him tomorrow.'

We sat down and I tasted my drink.

Bull said, 'Harry, don't take too many chances.'

'Chances?'

'Cullpepper. Don't give him an opening.'

'To do what?'

'Nail you. He will. He'll pin you to the nearest door. Give him half a chance—'

'What the hell for?'

'I dunno.' Bull looked worried. 'This job you do. I don't get it. I don't even know whether it's legal.'

'Certainly it's legal.'

'Just that—y'know—I don't know anybody else who's a detective who isn't in the force. Okay, movies. On TV. Maybe in books. But in real life.'

'It is "real life".'

'Yeah, but—y'know—it seems—'

'I know. Odd.' I grinned, sipped at the cider and wiped the moustache of froth from my top lip with the back of my hand. I said, 'Bull, it's not illegal. Not even shady. It's a perfectly honest profession. Look it up in the Yellow Pages.'

'Yeah, maybe—but—'

'Ex-coppers. Quite a few go into the

investigation business. In the capital—every city—it's big business, Bull. Okay, in books—in films—on TV—they're either crooks under another name or they spend their time making the cops look like so many bananas. It's not like that. It's a job. Get into the big time and it's a damn *good* job. Well paid. Big perks.' I grinned and added, 'When *I* get there we'll throw a party. With you as guest of honour.'

*   *   *

Detective Sergeant Owen Cullpepper had a fancy name. He had an equally fancy temper. The day they recruited him into the force reason and good sense were on extended sick leave. He was everything a copper should *not* be. He was an embarrassment to those who held higher rank than he did. He was an embarrassment to those who held *lower* rank than he did. And, to the rest of the world he was a prolonged and never ending pain in the arse.

He rang me at three o'clock next morning.

I rubbed the sleep out of my eyes, and said, 'Yeah?'

'Thompson?'

I should have recognised the bawl that was his voice, but I was not yet fully awake.

I said, 'Yeah, Thompson. Who's that?'

71

'Detective Sergeant Cullpepper—*that's who.*

'What the hell are you ringing at this time about?'

'I left word.'

'Eh?'

'To contact me. To get in touch. I left word.'

'You left—'

'With Adams. I told him I wanted to see you.'

'Hey, Cullpepper.' The clown's early-morning arrogance was breath-taking. I snapped, 'Tomorrow, boyo. Right? I'll find time to—'

'*Now!*'

'Why the hell—'

'I'm not asking favours, Thompson. I'm giving instructions.'

'What the hell—'

'You either come, or I fetch.'

I frowned and said, 'Do you have the weight necessary to make that brand of mouth noise?' I was backing down a little. Cullpepper's tone was even more mad-bull than usual. I added, 'You'd *better* have the weight, friend.'

'You'll know,' he warned. 'Stay at home and I—personally—will be round to shake the dew from your own, private rose petals.'

That was the way Cullpepper talked. Red-neck and full-bore nasty. Nor was he too human not to screw up the truth as justification for his words—or his deeds, come to that.

I returned the receiver, pulled on some

clothes and hurried through the cold, deserted streets to the police station.

A middle-aged constable at the public counter was expecting me. He sucked his nicotine-stained moustache and grunted, 'Thompson?'

'Of that ilk,' I admitted.

'CID Office.' He jerked his head. 'Up the stairs, then first on the left.'

'I know the way.'

'Cullpepper's expecting you.'

I took time off to light a cigarette, then made my way towards the stairs.

It was a very modern police station. A divisional headquarters of the county force. It claimed to have been 'architecturally designed'. This meant that it was all angles, corners and straight lines. Strip lighting was every few yards, and all the strips were lit. All shadows had been banished and, with the polished parquet floors and the gloss-painted walls, it had the look and feel of an off-beat operating theatre. Or maybe a high-class morgue. Maybe a cross between the two. Other than the copper at the counter and the waiting Cullpepper, I seemed to be the only occupant of the building. The only occupant of the *world*! It produced a feeling of nervousness. Like a well-made horror movie—hokum, but it just might be true.

And, furthermore, when not caged or collared, Cullpepper enjoyed unsheathing his

73

claws and baring his fangs. That knowledge, plus the hour, plus the place did not make for much comfort and joy.

I walked through the CID Office, tapped on the door with 'DS' painted on its panels, turned the knob and entered. The man looked across from behind a desk only slightly bigger than the average dining table.

'You could come, after all?' It was a leer, not a smile. He added, 'What we *can* do when we try.'

'I did *not* volunteer.'

'Oh yes you did.' He nodded slowly. 'For once in your life you were wise.'

'Okay. Now, I'm here...' I left the question with an open end.

'The Super's idea.' He waved a hand. 'Sit down, Thompson. This may take some time.'

'The Super?' I lowered myself onto an uncomfortable cane-bottomed chair.

'Lyle.'

'I saw him earlier today.' I corrected myself and said, 'Earlier *yesterday*.'

'About bacon.' He closed the file he'd been working on. 'About piggies not going to market.'

'I explained it to Lyle.'

'He said.'

The bastard was playing with me, like a cat playing with an injured bird. The o'clock, the business of being dragged from sleep and having to walk through cold streets. It was

74

having an effect, and Cullpepper knew it. He was enjoying himself.

I repeated, 'I explained it to Lyle.'

'Uh-huh.'

'In that case—'

'Bristol.'

'Near Bristol,' I agreed. 'That's why the firm—'

'Motorway driving.'

'Yeah. Of course. That's why they were built. To—'

'About what time?'

'Eh?'

'On the motorway. From Bristol. What time?'

'Before midnight. After midnight. Long after midnight. It's a long drive. I was at a Service Area—the back of the journey broken—at around midnight.'

'The Forton Service Area?'

'Who knows?' I moved a shoulder. 'I don't use them too much. To me they're all the same.'

'They're *not* all the same.'

'*You* know. *I* don't.' He was the one asking the questions. I was there to give answers. If possible non-answers. I was not there to either argue or speculate.' I said, 'Is it important?'

'What did you have to eat?'

'I didn't eat.'

'To drink?'

'Or drink.'

'Just for a leak?'

75

'Not even that.'

'You stopped at a Service Area. You didn't eat. You didn't piss. Why stop?'

'I'd been driving long enough.'

'To stretch your legs?'

'No.'

'You've just said you were stiff. That's why you stopped, so you say.'

'When did I say that?'

'What?'

'That I was stiff?'

'Dammit, Thompson, you said—'

'I said I'd been driving too long. That's all. I'd watched headlights coming towards me— reflected in the mirror—too many headlights. I wasn't stiff. I wasn't hungry. My bladder was working fine. Just to give my eyes a rest. That's all.'

I squashed what was left of the cigarette into Cullpepper's desk ash-tray. It gave a pause to the quick-fire session. It gave me breathing space and time to think.

He was nudging his way towards questions I didn't want him to ask—but I was damned if I knew *why* I didn't want him to ask them.

He sneered, 'Just sitting there?'

If the words didn't call me a liar, the tone certainly did.

'Just sitting there,' I agreed.

That was as far as I went. The truth. Nothing but the truth. But not the *whole* truth, if only because it was none of his business. I still didn't

76

know why I'd been dragged from bed. Until I knew that I saw no good reason to cooperate.

'That's all a load of crap.' It was an expressionless remark. But it was made with soft conviction.

'Because you make a statement, that doesn't make that statement a fact, Cullpepper.'

'I have a rank.'

'Yeah. Me too. Mine's "Mister".'

'So innocent,' he mocked. 'Just sitting there. The small hours at a motorway Service Area. And you're just sitting there.'

'Sitting there,' I agreed. 'Wishing I was home.'

'Talking to nobody.'

'Not a soul.'

'Not even leaving the car.'

'It was a cold night.'

'You're a liar,' he breathed. 'You were seen.'

'No.' I shook my head.

'In the restaurant. In the self-service area.'

I shook my head again.

'Seen,' he insisted. 'By the staff. By two lorry drivers. I've been there. I've asked questions. I *know*. You bought coffee and tea. Two cups. One for yourself. One for the bimbo.'

'Which bimbo?'

I could feel the shift of sand under my feet. He said, 'The one with the injured hand.'

Again I shook my head.

'The bimbo who walked out on you.'

'The bimbo who *what*?'

'The bimbo you followed.'

'No.'

'Where is she, Thompson? What did you do with her?'

*   *   *

We were, of course, talking about different Service Areas. I was talking about the one near junction twelve. Cullpepper was talking about the one near junction thirty-three. We were missing each other by miles—and hours.

That knowledge put me a hand-span ahead of him. It gave me an edge and I tried to keep that edge.

I blinked a couple of times, tried to look sheepish, then said, 'Oh! You mean *that* woman?'

'That's the one we're talking about.'

'Who knows?' I shook my head and bent my lips into what I hoped was a smile. 'If something's happened to her—'

'You bet your sweet life, Thompson. That's why you're here.'

'She was upright and healthy when she left me.'

'Is that a fact?' he mocked.

'An injured hand.'

'How come? How injured?'

'I think she fell.'

'Where?'

'Before I picked her up.'

I was still dealing with strict truth. For Cullpepper's benefit I was tarting it up a little. He, in turn, was fishing around in waters I'd deliberately muddied.

'Only an injured hand?' he scorned.

'I bandaged it for her,' I said innocently.

'Bandaged it?'

'I used a salt shaker.'

'A pepper shaker,' he corrected.

'Was it? I didn't take too much notice.'

'Maybe before you killed her?' he suggested nastily.

I held my breath for a moment then, in as calm a voice as possible, I said, 'Use what few brains God gave you, Cullpepper. I didn't even *know* her. Why the hell should I kill her?'

'We think she's dead. We think she was a murder victim.'

'You "think"? *You*?' I allowed my lip to curl. 'That of itself is something of a minor miracle. Just don't rupture anything by trying to lift ideas that are too heavy for you.'

'Thompson.' He was fighting to pull a blinder and we both knew it. He rasped, 'Don't feed me crap. Not forever. You're here, in this office, because—'

'Because you think she's dead,' I cut in. 'Because—if she is dead—you think it *might* be murder.'

'Uh-huh.' He nodded.

'Don't go completely off your trolley, Cullpepper.'

79

'And don't you get too bloody stroppy, boy,' he snarled. 'You *hope* I'm wrong ... maybe. But I think I have the measure of you, Thompson.'

'You're "thinking" again,' I warned.

'I say she's dead. I say she's—'

'With a pipsqueak sergeant steering the enquiry?' He'd over-reached himself and he knew it, and I knew it. And he knew *I* knew it. I let him have the full blast of contempt. I sneered, 'You have me *there*, at the Service Area, my friend. That's all. That's as far as you go. You, and the whole damn force. One tiny hope in hell that I might have murdered her— one serious suggestion that she's *been* murdered—and this floor would be sagging under the weight of rank.'

I lighted a cigarette in the silence that followed. I'd stopped him. I'd made him re-align his sights. I could almost hear the wheels inside his skull moving into a new gear.

At last he said, 'You've lied, Thompson.'

'Is that a fact?'

'Since you walked through that bloody door, you've done little else but lie.'

'With you,' I reminded him, 'that is an occupational hazard. You are a detective sergeant. *Everybody* lies to detective sergeants. It's part of the game rules. Like leading with the left in a prize fight.'

'Not when it's murder.'

'What the—'

'Not if they have sense. Not when they're being—'

'You're punching all the wrong buttons, Cullpepper,' I snapped. 'We've decided. It's *not* murder. Not yet. All everything adds up to is some very personal nastiness on your part. For the sake of being an out-and-out bastard you've dragged me from my bed in the small hours. Do that—but, don't gripe if, for no good reason, I lie like the clappers. I'll take pleasure in lying. I'll give Ananias half a field start.'

'You were *there*.'

'I was at the Service Area,' I agreed. 'I was seen. Lorry drivers saw me. People behind the serving counter saw me. That's what you tell me. Great. Why not? I wasn't trying *not* to be seen.'

'Wrong Service Area, Thompson.'

'Wrong?'

'Wrong,' he repeated.

'Out of bounds? Is that what you're trying to say?'

'From Bristol,' he said, and his voice had a hate-filled edge.

'So?'

'Wrong Service Area. You leave the motorway at junction thirty-one.'

'Not last night.'

'Something *special* about last night?'

'I was with the Mason woman.'

'Eh?'

81

'That was her name. I thought I was taking her home. I was mistaken.'

'You *knew* her.' The way he pounced was pathetic.

'I picked her up.' I still wasn't lying ... strictly speaking. 'She wanted a lift. I obliged.'

'You know her name.'

'She *told* me her name. Mason. Mrs Kay Mason.'

'Nice,' he sneered.

'Civilised,' I countered.

'Where did you pick her up?'

'Another Service Area. South. Down the motorway.'

'Which one?'

'Who knows? They all look the same.'

'Come off it, Thompson.'

'I picked her up.' I chose my words carefully. No obvious lies. Only the truth—but perhaps a little twisted in the telling. I said, 'I stopped. Parked. She came towards me, then fell. That's when she broke her hand. She wanted junction thirty-three. That's where we were making for. But I thought it wise to stop off at a Service Area for repairs to her hand.'

'Just like that.'

The expression on Cullpepper's face was very ugly. It was that of a man who knows he's been beaten, and doesn't like being beaten.

'Just like that.' I nodded and hardened my tone. 'Take it. Throw it away. It's all I have to offer. Try to milk something more from it and I

82

yell for the nearest lawyer and chop you off at the knees.'

*　　　*　　　*

It was creeping up to five when I left the police station. There was a hard chill in the air and a pewter colour to the lightening sky over the rooftops of the town. I walked towards the prom as a deliberate, long-way-round route to my home base.

Cullpepper wasn't quite satisfied, but who cared about Cullpepper. I'd ducked, I'd weaved and I'd boxed clever. But I hadn't lied. If the roof caved in I could stand in a witness box and claim to have told only the truth. Innuendoes and emphases had done the rest.

Kay Mason had been a pick-up. One of the floozies who stand expectantly at every slip-road leading from the Service Areas onto the motorways. I'd offered her a lift. She'd given the impression of being slightly better than the average cab-happy bimbo. The object of a mildly naughty exercise had been to find some no-questions-asked hotel, somewhere. Not too far from her home. And, in a strange but comfortable bed, I'd expected to experience carnal enjoyment.

Cullpepper had swallowed it.

He had the right type of mind. The leer as he'd asked unnecessary questions had been proof of the dirty pictures building up in his imagination. The slight gleam of his eyes. The quick moistening of his lips.

He'd built up his own scenario. All I'd had to do was nod and make noises of agreement.

He'd ended by saying, 'Right. Be warned. Keep yourself available. I'll knock out a report for the Lancashire crowd. They might want to ask you a few more questions.'

That, then, was the state of play ... and, for some God-given reason, I yearned to shove my own fingers deeper into the pie.

Maybe because of Cullpepper. Maybe because of the Mason woman. Maybe because I'd read too many private-eye yarns. Maybe *anything*. Or, maybe because I was parting company with what few marbles I claimed still to have; equating real life with the Phil-Marlowe-Sunset-Strip crap every non-official investigator has to carry around on his back. I had this gut feeling. That, well hidden behind the non-answers I'd fed to Cullpepper, a whole swarm of not-too-obvious questions were waiting for some curiosity-minded clown to stir them around.

I was tempted.

I walked slowly along a snow-dusted and deserted promenade. I stared out to sea until a frost-touched north-westerly brought tears to my eyes. I smoked a couple of cigarettes and coughed a little. I tried logic in an attempt to drop a safety curtain on crazy ideas milling around in my head. Logic hadn't a hope in hell.

84

It couldn't compete with the remnants of what had once been moderate success in the field of investigative journalism.

I fell.

I was going to nose around in a lot of none-of-my-business. I was, perhaps, going to stumble into outsized trouble. Giant trouble. It was more than possible. I tried to figure out ways of softening the crash if I came unstuck. None of the ways had much hope. This trick did not admit of a safety net. One slip and I was likely to have a snapped neck ... and that, too, was a gut feeling.

I take careful note of gut feelings. So often they have proved to be right.

I showered, dressed then went down to *The Wine Bibber* for an early, before-opening-time breakfast, English style. Then, having given her a ring to warn her I was on my way, I climbed into the car and drove to Liz's apartment.

*   *   *

Liz. Let me tell you the truth about Liz. She is a glutton for punishment. She won't divorce me and I can't bring myself to divorce her. Ours is the classic impossible-to-live-with-can't-live-without marriage. We each favour the wrong things. From music to dress sense. From food to literature. You name it, if one likes it the chances are the other will count it as crap.

But, because she is a doll and quite unique, she saw me through a mental crack-up brought on by digging too deeply for copy and doing without sleep in order to meet a deadline.

After that, we separated—and discovered we were still crazy about each other. But, we were 'adult'. We were 'modern'. We reached a working agreement.

No alimony. We each kept our own place, but we remained great friends. As great friends, and when the urge demanded, we spent the night together. No strings. Complete trust. We even kidded ourselves it wasn't love. Simple, basic, natural lust. Controlled lechery, if you will. But safe and satisfying—which in this age of sexual antics of dubious nature is no small thing.

We were surprised to discover a deep, mutual respect for each other. More than that. It was a respect far in excess of that demanded by a mere wedding band and an authenticated marriage certificate.

Liz had worked her way up to be junior partner in one of the town's leading solicitor's offices. All her valves and cylinders functioned very smoothly and, given a free hand, she could out-smart anybody I knew.

She listened to my story, smoked her first cigarette of the day and sipped black coffee. She listened without interrupting and that, as a woman, made her very unusual.

When I'd finished, she took a deep draw on

the cigarette, exhaled, then asked, 'Coffee?'

'I've had breakfast at Bull's place.'

'Does Bull know about all this?'

'He knows what you know—more or less.'

'Which means?'

'About Cullpepper wanting to see me. Beyond that, nothing.'

'What does he think?'

'He thinks I should go to Lyle. Tell him everything.'

'Bull has brains. You haven't.'

'For Christ's sake! Cullpepper was bluffing.'

'Of course.'

'In that case, why should I—'

'Lyle isn't bluffing. Lyle never bluffs.'

'Lyle?' I couldn't keep pace with her thinking.

'Cullpepper sends for you—fine ... but *why*? Because Lyle thinks you might be able to help ... but help *what*? A possible murder enquiry? A possible abduction? Because you're a possible witness? Come on, lover boy. Use your brains. If it's *that* important a man like Lyle doesn't slide that sort of enquiry on to a yo-yo like Cullpepper.'

I said 'Ah!' because, put that way, it was so blindingly obvious—and also so blindingly baffling.

'I don't think murder,' she said, with finality. 'I don't think abduction.' She looked a question, then asked, 'What?'

'I thought—y'know...' I moved my hands

87

in an aimless gesture.

'What?' she repeated.

'A motor car, maybe. Something like that. Like they tried at the other Service Area.'

'A deliberate run-down?'

'It's a possibility. That's what I thought.'

'But Cullpepper didn't say? Didn't even hint?'

'Cullpepper asked questions,' I growled. Cullpepper played at conversational tag. He didn't offer information. He isn't the sort.'

She sipped coffee, enjoyed cigarette smoke then, very slowly, said, 'Okay. Your lady companion of last night.'

'Not *last* night. The night *before* last.'

'Whenever. Let's assume something happened to her. I don't think murder. I don't think abduction. But *something*. You were there. The police have questioned you, naturally. You have nothing to do with what happened. You know nothing. Absolutely nothing.' There was a pause, a drag on the cigarette, then, 'Why are you *here*, lover boy? Why consult me, and what about? What goes on under that thatch of yours?'

'It's—er...' What I was contemplating didn't make too much sense. It was even more difficult to explain. I tried again. 'It's a thought I have. An idea. That's all.'

'A thought?'

'Yeah. It seemed like a good idea. It *still* seems like a good idea.'

'What does?'

'It's just that—well—y'know … maybe somebody's trying to frame me.'

'*Frame* you?'

'Well—that's what I—'

'What on earth for?'

'I don't know. Just that—'

'In heaven's name, where did you dig *that* notion from?'

'It's possible.'

'Frame you for *what*?'

'I don't know. I have this gut feeling. It's—'

'It's indigestion, that's all.'

'Something's happened.' I felt my chin jut a little. 'I'd like to know what.'

'It's none of your damn business. It's—'

'I've nothing on the books at the moment.'

'Oh, no!' Her mouth opened and she stared.

'I'm not going to break any laws.'

'You're out of your mind.'

'Just ask around. Just—'

'You are a private investigator. A shamus. The police aren't too keen on your kind. You're not even big. You're not affiliated to any regional, much less national, network. I hate to remind you of this, but you're small. Minuscule. *Nothing*.'

'Well, thank you kindly.'

'And if you mess around with what doesn't concern you, Lyle will chew you up and spit you out. He won't even taste you.'

'I'm not thinking of—'

Ah, but you are, boy. You *are*. I know you. I know you too well. You read too many American novels. Crime novels. Gumshoe novels. You think it's for real.'

'Over there it is for real. Over there—'

'Over there!' She waved the hand holding the cigarette. In her own way she was getting spitting mad. 'I doubt if it's for real, even in America. But what if it is? We're not "over there". We're here. In Rogate-on-Sands. And *here* it's not allowed. Any suggestion of obstructing the police in their—'

'Who the hell said anything about obstructing the—'

'That's what you're talking about, boy. Don't kid yourself. Don't kid *me*. That Cullpepper sent for you proves *something*. And if you mess around—'

'To know why,' I snapped. 'That's all. To know why she was nearly run down. Why she's disappeared. For God's sake, Liz, I'm not a child. I'm long-gone potty-trained. I need to know things. When I'm involved, I need to know.'

'You'll do it.' She drew deeply on the cigarette. 'It's crazy, but you'll *do* it.'

I nodded.

'Yeah, and you'll buy trouble *doing* it.'

The last words rode on what was little more than a sigh. She drew on the cigarette again, then stood up and carried her cup into the kitchen. There was an air of finality about her movements. I knew her well enough to know the signs, and I was sorry. I'd hoped she would understand, and maybe help. There wasn't a chance. To save further argument I followed her lead. I straightened from the table and left the apartment.

*   *   *

I passed junction twelve and watched for the entrance to the Service Area. This time I was travelling south. The same motorway, a different direction. The sun was up there, above my left shoulder somewhere, but nobody could see it. The clouds were too thick, and they were fat and heavy with snow. Some of it was drifting earthwards, and had been all night, and I mentally cursed myself for not taking the advice of both Liz and Bull.

I flicked the wiper switch and two clear arcs appeared in what might have been mistaken for a splintered windscreen. I hoisted the heater up a couple of notches. Inside the car I didn't feel cold, but I felt I *should* have felt cold. Snow has that effect on me.

I tried to use what little brains I had left. The trick was to keep in the fast lane and the overtaking lane. That way I dodged as much rear-wheel spray as possible. Especially from the heavy stuff. It would, I knew, build up. Once the gritters had done their work, the whole of the motorway—north and south lanes—would carry a head-high mist of khaki gunge, and the gunge would stick to windscreens and rear windows and driving would become a concentrated, eye-aching torture.

And I was there driving through the muck, with an even worse return journey coming up, primarily because Liz and Bull had said I shouldn't.

Had I been anybody other than Harry Thompson I would have counted myself the complete, pearl-encrusted no-holds-barred prat!

Meanwhile the snow was getting heavier and, as always, the illusion was that I was driving through an Arctic blizzard as it flew at the windscreen.

The three-bar Service Area sign came up and I eased the car into the slow lane. I kept the trafficators flashing, passed the two-bar sign, then the one-bar sign and finally I eased off the motorway and onto the slip road. The Service Area was (I noticed) a *Welcome Break* outfit. The Service Area also had a name. Michael Wood. There was plenty of room in the park. I drove as near as I could to the restaurant complex then, having locked the car, I ran for the steps and made for the bridge.

On the north-bound half of the complex I made my way into the eating area and checked the people who were servicing the people who were eating. The collectors of litter from the tables. The servers of food. The cleaners of floors. I was surprised to realise just how many members of staff were needed to fill the bellies of travellers going north.

I noted a guy who looked nondescript, wasn't eating, wasn't drinking and who gave the impression of having some authority. I walked over to him, and asked, 'You in charge here?'

'Could be. Who wants to know?'

Instead of answering his question, I asked another half-question.

'Last night—about midnight—a woman left here.'

For a split second his expression showed annoyance—then mild shock—and, finally, he gaped at me as if I was slightly stupid, but said nothing.

'She was wearing a brown overcoat. Light brown.'

He hesitated a moment, then offered, 'I wasn't here. Nobody on duty now was here last night.'

'Oh!'

'They'll come on duty later this evening.'

'It follows,' I murmured. 'I should have guessed.'

'They won't tell you.' He seemed to be offering information, crumb at a time. He added, 'Unless you're local police, of course.'

'I'm not police.'

'I didn't think so.'

93

'No?'

'They'd know. About nobody being on now who was on last night.'

'Ah!'

'They wouldn't be wasting time asking.' He lowered himself onto a chair, gave a tight little smile, then said, 'Pursuing husband? Eh?'

'What?' I stared.

'I don't mind,' he said, airily. 'It has absolutely nothing to do with me.'

'Good, because I don't even know what the hell you're talking about.' I sat down on another chair at the same table, then said, 'At least answer *that* question.'

'Pursuing husbands.' He moved one shoulder in what I think was meant to be a very blasé, couldn't-care-less shrug. 'This motorway. Particularly *this* motorway. This and the M5. Devon to Carlisle, see? Then dual carriageway all the way to Glasgow. A direct route to the Scottish motorway system, if that's what you want.'

'And do you?' I asked.

'It's a great escape route for bored wives, when they take off with their toy boys and fancy men.'

'Gretna Green,' I smiled.

'Not with that sort.' There was a sneer in his voice, and a curl of scorn on his lips. 'This isn't the age of romance—if there even *was* one.

'And, of course, if—as you suggest—they're already married.'

'But not to each other.'

I took cigarettes from my pocket, placed one between my lips then tossed the still-opened packet onto the table. He accepted the silent invitation and helped himself. I thumbed a lighter and held the flame, first to the end of his cigarette, then to the end of mine.

It was all part of an oddball pantomime. We were, it seemed, indulging in a mild, verbal duel. But why? What was it he didn't want to tell me? What was it he wanted me to tell *him*?

I tried to get the timing right. I said, 'There was an AA man around.'

'Where?'

'Here.'

'When?'

'When the woman left the complex for her car. When she left this restaurant.'

'No. No AA man.'

'I was there,' I insisted. 'I'm not guessing. I saw him. He was by the entrance.'

'No.' He shook his head. He drew on the cigarette, exhaled, then said, 'The AA man responsible for this area is away. In the Med somewhere. On his honeymoon.'

'In that case—'

'The man who covers for him is in a sick bed. Flu.'

'In that case—' I began again.

'The second long-stop only comes for emergencies. He doesn't cover this stretch. Ever! He stays in this area for as short a time as

95

possible. He wouldn't call in here. It's as much as his job's worth.'

'No AA man?'I turned it into a questioning sigh.

'Gamble on it.'

We sat and smoked for a few moments. He was, I think, waiting for me to say something. I would have happily obliged, had I been able to think of something to say.

In a tone that suggested he wasn't too interested in my answer, he said, 'You're *not* a pursuing husband?'

'She's an acquaintance.'

'Is that all?' His eyes told me he didn't believe me, and I hoped my eyes told him I didn't give a damn.

'Name of Kay Mason,' I added.

'That's a nice name.'

'She's a nice woman, and she's missing.'

'Missing?'

'Not where she should be.'

'That must be worrying.'

'A little worrying,' I agreed.

'Been missing long?'

'She was here.' He was probing like the clappers, but pretending *not* to probe. I didn't mind, so I answered him.

'When?' he asked.

'A couple of nights ago.'

'Kay Mason?'

'The AA man saw her.'

'He didn't.' He gave a quick, hard smile. 'He

wasn't here, remember?'

'So you say.'

'And you're *not* a police officer.'

'So *you* say,' I repeated.

'No, *you* said.'

'Ah!'

'Mr—er...'

'Thompson.'

'Ah, yes. You mentioned.'

'Did I?'

'You also said "last night". Now, it's "a couple of nights ago".'

'Within the last week,' I fenced.

'That's not very precise.'

'Precision isn't my long suit.'

We were both fishing for answers and, at the same time, trying to dodge a way round questions. Neither of us was getting far.

I tried a blinder for size. I said, 'She was trying to contact Hanbury.'

'Hanbury?' he blinked.

'Dick Hanbury. Surely you know Hanbury. He works here.'

'Oh, *that* Hanbury?'

'She came here to see him.'

'Did she?' He raised his eyebrows.

'We haven't seen her since.'

'It must be worrying.'

'A little. It's why I'm here.'

'Have you seen *him* yet? Hanbury, I mean.'

'Not yet.'

'Ah!'

'I thought I'd ask *you* first.'

'Tell him.' He pushed himself upright. 'Tell him it's okay. That *I* say he can answer questions.'

'And you?' I smiled.

'Eh?'

'You won't be there?'

'I'll join you.' He squashed out his cigarette. 'I have a few small jobs to see to, on the south-bound side. I'll join you later.'

'I'll wait,' I lied.

He left the eating area and through the window I watched the glass-sided bridge spanning the six lanes of the motorway. I smoked my cigarette, gazed at the gently falling snow and waited. I waited all of twenty minutes. But he didn't cross the bridge.

* * *

I'd eaten. And why not? I had more than fifty miles of driving ahead of me, and it was still snowing. Driving south had been a mistake. Driving back north, in this weather, was going to be a distinct and self-inflicted pain in the arse.

I sat for a few minutes and allowed the meal time to digest. Then I strolled to the serving counter and spoke to the woman handling the tea and coffee.

I said, 'The manager. I'd like a word with him, please.'

'Yes, luv.' She busied herself for a few moments, filling cups and teapots from various urns, then she spoke to another server who was squeezing past her.

She smiled at me and said, 'I've sent word. She'll be with you in a minute.'

'She?'

'It's the manageress who's on duty at the moment.'

'Fine.' I jerked my head. 'I'll have another tea, then I'll get out of your way. I'll be at the corner table. Okay?'

'I'll tell her, luv.'

I took myself and the cup of tea to the corner table and waited. I did not have to wait long. The manageress was small, trim, neatly dressed and carried a worried half-smile on her face.

She said, 'Is there something wrong, sir?'

'Nothing wrong.' I grinned reassurance, then motioned with my spare hand. I sipped tea, then said, 'If you've time to sit down for a few minutes. Some questions I'd like to ask about a few nights ago.'

The half-smile turned to a puzzled frown, but she sat down.

I fished a card from my breast pocket, handed it to her, then said, 'That's me. The Thompson Detective Bureau. I'm Harry Thompson. I have no official authority, and you can tell me to blow at any time.'

'Why should I?'

She read the card a few times. She seemed

surprised to learn that private detectives actually live outside book covers and away from cinema and TV screens. She wasn't unique in this. She was merely one of a large army.

I said, 'About midnight, a couple of nights ago. Somebody tried to run down a lady as she left here for the car park. I wondered whether—'

'I wasn't on duty.'

'Oh. In that case—'

'But I was told about it. The AA patrolman apparently saw it happen.'

'The AA patrolman?'

'Yes.' She nodded.

'There is an AA patrolman?'

'Of course. He saw it happen, and—'

'He *isn't* on his honeymoon?'

She blinked, then stared.

I pressed on, and said, 'He *isn't* off duty sick?'

'Not that I know of. He calls in, when he's passing. He was certainly on duty earlier today. He was in the kitchen, drinking tea.'

She was a bright lady. She realised that, somewhere in our exchange, our wires had become badly crossed, and she waited for me to uncross them.

I told her what had happened about an hour or so back—about the nondescript guy with the air of authority—and she smiled resignedly.

She said, 'I know. We've seen him hanging around.'

'Doing what?'

'Apparently waiting for something.'

'Or somebody.'

She said, 'Fred mentioned it to the police.'

'Fred?'

'The AA patrolman.'

'Oh.'

'And about the other night. Two cars were damaged.'

'I know. A Ford and a Honda.'

'The police don't want to know.'

'Eh?'

'Fred reported it to the motorway patrol officers.'

'Uh-huh.' I nodded my understanding and murmured, 'It didn't happen on the Queen's highway.'

'That's what they said.'

'Therefore not—officially—an "accident".'

'It sounds so *silly*.'

'It *is* silly,' I assured her. 'The law is sometimes very silly. Added to which, some policemen are *very* silly.'

She looked sad. Disappointed. Like a kid who's dropped his toffee apple in the mud. It was as if I'd disillusioned her.

I said, 'About the guy I've just spoken to? The guy who seems to be waiting.'

'Nothing.' She made a tiny, hand-spreading gesture. 'Same thing. He's doing nothing

101

illegal. Members of the public *can* arrange to meet here. It's private property. Nothing to do with the police as long as he behaves himself.'

It was the old you-win-I-lose set-up beloved of every legal nit-picker under the sun. As always, the cops were carrying the blame, but it wasn't their fault. They just happened to be handy. They also happened to have board backs.

I knew the woman, Kay Mason, had been almost chopped.

I knew that two perfectly good motor cars had been dented.

But (strictly speaking) at that moment the law was not on this planet.

I asked, 'Do you employ somebody called Hanbury? Dick Hanbury?'

'No.' She shook her head. 'Nobody of that name. Why do you ask?'

'Just double-checking,' I sighed. 'That's all.'

*   *   *

I seemed to have been at that damn Service Area a small lifetime. I'd seen people come and watched the same people go. I knew exactly which were 'Smoking' tables and which were 'No Smoking' tables. I knew the view from every window, the pattern of the tiles in the john and the make of the condoms for sale at the vending machine. I'd long since reached the stage of a nod and a smile from the tea lady. I wasn't far from being included in the inventory.

I pushed myself upright and decided it was time I returned to the south-bound side of the motorway, collected my car, drove to the next junction and then started the homeward trudge to my own base and my own cot.

I walked out of the eating hall, through the foyer, down the shallow steps—and almost immediately I saw the car.

Her car!

I had absolutely no doubts. It was there, alongside where I'd parked a couple of nights before, on my way north. There was no snow on the park surface within its four wheels. No tyre tracks led up to it. More than that—the clincher, as far as I was concerned—a splinter of remembrance returned; the memory of reversing into the gap, and the glimpse of a pillar-box-red Porsche. You don't see Porsches waiting for the green at every traffic light. They are not scarce enough to be *unique*, but they are undoubtably thin on the ground.

I walked over to it and touched the radiator with the back of my hand. The metal was as cold as the snow falling onto it. I took a handkerchief from my pocket, covered my fingers and tried the doors. They were all locked. So was the boot. There was nothing on the seats, or on the dashboard shelf.

A voice said, 'Put it down, lad, before you scorch your fingers.'

103

It was a hard, no-nonsense voice. The sort of voice that doesn't say things twice.

I began, 'I was only—'

'Shut it!' The second voice was just as hard and pitched maybe a tone or so higher.

Neither voice was that of a pansy.

I didn't turn round. I didn't look. I didn't even *want* to look—in case what I saw scared me even more. Quite suddenly I decided I was no hero. I was merely a nosey bastard who, by this time, was fervently wishing he *wasn't* a nosey bastard.

Two fingers—a forefinger and a middle finger—were pushed down my collar, at the nape of the neck. Then the fingers clenched and the fist was turned. It was an old police trick. If, like me, you were civilised enough to wear a tie, it made a very effective do-it-yourself garrotte.

The first voice said, 'You're a mug, Thompson. You never learn.'

The second voice said, 'The hints were big enough, boy. Don't complain.'

'What the hell—'

That was as far as I got. My hands had already gone to my neck in an attempt to ease the constriction. The grip at the nape tightened, fractionally, the arm beyond the fist straightened and my face hit the upper bodywork of the Porsche.

It wasn't much different from being smacked in the puss with a brick. Coloured flashes swam before my eyes and, for a

104

moment, I wasn't part of this world.

I was allowed to slump alongside the car, and when I recovered my senses the apes responsible for the quick going-over had vanished.

I gulped air for a few moments and wanted to puke, but didn't. I stayed on all fours, pending the slowing down of the merry-go-round, and, while I was down there, I admired the pretty patterns made in the snow, with the gore from my suffering hooter.

I also felt very sorry for myself.

Maybe less than a hundred years later, I wobbled to my feet. I dabbed at my throbbing nose with a handkerchief which soon became soaked. After another century or so the bleeding seemed to ease, and, as it eased, I grew shivery and damp with the snow. I crossed the footbridge, collected my own car, left the Service Area and joined the traffic heading south, prior to switching direction at junction fourteen.

*　　　*　　　*

I muttered, '*Dammit to hell!*'

I was talking to myself. It might, indeed, have been the first sign of an oncoming senility but, as far as I was concerned, it was also a means of fighting the sheer boredom of motorway driving at dusk. It was certainly a deal better, and more interesting than some of the crap being churned out by various radio stations.

Therefore I muttered, '*Dammit to hell!*' then continued, '*I have, of course, taken too much for granted. She was not running for cover. Not the way I figured she was. She was running for the Porsche. For the safety of her own car. And why not? Put a Porsche up against almost any other car on the road and it's a "no contest" situation. Climb behind the wheel of a Porsche. Enjoy a few slices of luck prior to hitting the motorway lanes. After that you're home and dry.*'

The car swayed as a high-loader overtook on the inside lane. The dumb bastard behind the wheel was not only in the wrong lane, he was also going too fast for the weather conditions. He was a mobile accident impatient to happen and, when it *did* happen, some poor slob might not crawl his way from the twisted metal. I sent a quick prayer aloft—if it *had* to happen, let it be the prat behind the wheel of the high-loader.

'*That was the scenario,*' I mumbled, '*but it didn't come off. The ice underfoot made the car skid. It also made the Mason woman skid. That was why the bad guys missed. That was why the cops were waiting at the Service Area.* (And I had little doubt that they *were* cops.) *Waiting for her to reclaim her car. Waiting for* her. *And* that, *Thompson old buddy, old pal, doesn't make too much sense.*'

I swung left, into the slow lane, then onto the slip road. Then right and right again, round the roundabout. Then left and down the feed slip road and, at last, onto the north-bound carriageway and heading towards home territory.

'*And Harry Thompson, old pal, old friend, old chum, you are the world's most over-sized prat.*' I mumbled away to myself. To kill the tedium, and also to drag my mind away from the aches and the discomforts. '*A good-looking woman, with an injured hand. And you thought she was running for cover. To dodge murderous pursuers. And you, old friend, old buddy, old mate, couldn't even mind your own cotton-picking business. You were in there, nose at the ready. And dammit you're* still *in there, long snout twitching away like crazy. Boy, can you soak up punishment!*'

Around me, the heavy stuff was still pushing north, for Liverpool. Some of the booze joints had been open all day and, already, idiots on wheels had been made even more suicidal by the intake of throat-varnish. They were weaving and swerving, playing homicidal Catch-Me-If-You-Can in all three lanes of the motorway. The gritters had been out, and the brown slush plastered the windscreen and the rear window where wipers couldn't reach. Headlights coming towards me and tail-lights going away from me made an eye-blinking mix of moving fairy lamps spinning around in the gloom and the still-falling snow.

'*Think about it, Thompson old buddy, old*

charmer. Use what little grey matter the good Lord slipped under the dandruff. She was on this motorway. This *motorway*. Travelling north. From where? From London? From Bristol? From Wales? From the West Country? Up the M1, then branch left on the M6? Maybe from the M5?

'She stopped. That's one thing we know for sure. Maybe the only thing we know for sure. She'd stopped at a Service Area. The Service Area you've just left. Okay ... why? For a meal? For a leak? For what?

'She'd driven some distance, right? A meal, or a leak equates with a long journey, either interrupted or completed. It also equates with another long journey yet to come. That's it, Thompson, my old croney, my old mastermind. She'd come a long way. She was going a long way.

'Great, but from where? And how long is "Long"? Because "long", my old chum, my old hoppo, is a long long way.

'Think about it. Fillet it.

'She was driving a Porsche. Not a Mini. Not a souped-up Robin. A Porsche. So it wasn't cramp that made her stop. It wasn't a headache from road noise. With a Porsche, you can drive all day without coming up for air. It wasn't juice she was short of. The pumps are always on the way out of a Service Area, so it wasn't juice. Correction—it wasn't only juice. Some other reason with, maybe a fill-up as a second thought.'

108

Talking to myself was crazy, but I was not alone. Everybody does it. Those one-liners you could have corked up some smart-arse with, maybe a week ago. They always come too late to be used. When you're alone. When you're in the shower. When you're waiting for a train. When you're driving in traffic.

Me? I didn't go in for too many one-liners. *I played at Sherlock Holmes and Doctor Watson. I made a simple two-and-two add up to a damn sight more than four.*

'She wanted junction thirty-three, after a particularly long journey. No prompting. That's what she asked for. Not thirty-two. Not thirty-four. Thirty-three. Fine. But forget the west of Glasson crap. Take Bull's word for it. Only water west of Glasson. Nevertheless, she still latched onto the name "Glasson". She still asked for junction thirty-three. Why? Why else other than that she knows the district.'

A gritter came towards me, on the south-bound carriageway. In the falling snow it looked like something from science fiction. Orange lights flashing at each corner. A yellow, rotating light on top of the cab. Dipped headlights. The spread from a small floodlight illuminating two weather-coated workmen feeding the spreader. The broadcast salt—like so much dirty rice being thrown at an off-beat wedding—giving the whole set-up a broad slipstream of filth. Like something from science fiction, definitely.

'Think about it, Thompson. Think about it.
Use that incisive, analytical brain of yours. That
massive intelligence. That stop-at-nothing
mentality. Junction thirty-three. Remember?
Where do you go from junction thirty-three?
Think! Remember! You know that neck of the
woods. So you claim. You're no stranger to the
North-West. You're on a motorway—this
motorway—*the M6. You're coming up to*
junction thirty-three. You intend to leave *the*
motorway at that junction. Okay, bird-brain,
where might *you be going?'*

I was, of course, being a little crazy. Maybe
more than a little. I had pain in my face and my
head. Behind the eyes. At the nape of the neck.
Not the sharp, biting pain that keeps you
awake and alert. But an overall dull, throbbing
ache which merely seemed to add to my
tiredness. I therefore argued with myself—
played a mad game of Who-Killed-Cock-
Robin—in an effort to make time and space
pass more quickly—even though it might be
only fractionally more quickly.

'Where might anybody be going, from the M6
and junction thirty-three? Where might *they be*
going, Thompson? The A6. Where else? All the
other linked roads at that junction are
unclassified. Little more than dirt-tracks. That,
old buddy, is the peculiarity of junction thirty-
three. All unclassified roads, except for the A6.
Thereafter, the M6 and the A6 run north,
alongside each other. Past junction thirty-four.

All the way to junction thirty-five.

'Get it? A stretch of motorway. It's main purpose to carry north-bound and south-bound traffic past the vehicular balls-up at Lancaster. But, going north, if you want Lancaster, you leave the motorway at junction thirty-three. Join the old A6. If you want Lancaster. There's very few other places to go to from that junction.

'Easy, when you know how. Figure it out. It's like taking toffee from a blind child. Lancaster. And Lancaster hugs Morecambe to its breast, and Morecambe is tucked away in the same bed as Heysham, and Heysham runs a regular, daily ferry to Ireland.

'Ergo! The Mason dame was on the run, making for Ireland, and somebody wanted to stop her from reaching there.

'And Thompson, my old cock-sparrow, that means you have won yourself a coconut.'

I was tired of talking to myself. It was self-kidology ... maybe. Either way, I hadn't a hope in hell of finding how right I was—or how wrong I was—and it was all a waste of time.

After that, it merely took patience and the fine tuning of the heater controls to keep me warm enough for comfort, but not warm enough to make me nod off. The impression was that I would be driving forever, that the snow would be whipping towards the windscreen forever, and that nobody would ever again dip their bloody headlights.

And I was an idiot for doing the coppers'

111

work for them.

And I would never, ever do it again.

*   *   *

It was nice being home. It was a bit of a dump; it was untidy and, if somebody had twisted my arm enough, I might have agreed that it was a poor apology for what I'd once had with Liz. But, despite its drawbacks, it was home and, to me, it was nice.

I fed a Dorsey tape into the stereo, then switched things on. The kettle boiled for instant coffee. The bars of the electric fire began to glow and pump sweet and cosy heat into the apartment.

I unlaced my shoes, loosened my tie, flopped onto the divan and, taking most things into consideration, figured myself to be a fairly fortunate guy.

At the level of the flat windows the yellow, sodium street-lighting gave the illusion of warmth. The snow was floating down in florin-sized flakes, and the yellow wash made the flakes look pure and beautiful. In the background Dorsey's trombone was like silk as it took a cheap, Tin-Pan-Alley number and gave it a sweet magic it didn't deserve.

It was one of those moments.

The kettle boiled. I brewed myself coffee, then relaxed and opened the newspaper I'd brought up from the hall.

It was a national, and it headlined the latest nastiness in the Big City. Camden Town and Highgate were, apparently, the latest battleground for the long-running, North-of-the-River gang war. It boiled down to the usual thing. Protection and prostitution; the everyday sort of crap that soils every major city on earth; louts whose forté is putting various frighteners on people.

I glanced at the large print, then turned the page. I had more than enough troubles of my own.

In the background Dorsey moved into the neat, hiccupy introduction to *Sunny Side Of The Street*, and the telephone bell completely wrecked the happy sweetness of the sound.

I lifted the receiver and gave my number.

A man's voice said, 'Thompson? Harry Thompson?'

'Speaking.'

I'd heard the voice somewhere but, for the moment, couldn't put a name or a face to it. Then it clicked. The man—that very nondescript man—I'd mistakenly thought was the manager at the Service Area.

I asked, 'Who is it?'

'We spoke.' The creep was giving nothing away.

'When?'

'Earlier today.'

'I don't recall.' Two could play at conversational hide-and-seek.

'About the AA man.'

'Who wasn't there?'

'That's the one.'

'But who, in fact, *was*?'

A soft chuckle came over the wire.

'Who the hell are you?' I demanded.

'A friend.' He didn't sound too friendly. He didn't sound *anything*. He was using a flat, emotionless voice. He said, 'A friend giving good advice.'

'Do I *need* advice?'

'Put your life on it.'

'Really?'

'Literally.'

'If,' I mused, 'I knew who was proffering the advice—'

'That isn't important.'

'That's where we differ—"friend".'

'Simple advice, Thompson. Just drop it.'

'Drop it?'

'These Nosey Parker habits you've cultivated. They mean trouble.'

'Threats? Is that it?'

'I've already said—advice.'

'And if I told you to stuff your advice?'

'That wouldn't be very wise.'

'No?'

'Believe me.'

This time I chuckled, but it was a false and forced chuckle. I said, 'As I see things, you are a deliberately anonymous person. Right?'

'Right.'

'Without even the simple guts—the common gumption—to give a clue to his name?'

'Not *stupid* enough.'

'So-o ... why should I take any notice of anything a character like that has to say?'

'Thompson. I think you're being very silly.'

'Am I?'

'That is my considered opinion.'

'Assuming I ask, of course—but I haven't asked.'

'Just don't complain. That's all.'

'So far, I've had nothing to complain *about*.'

'Don't say we didn't warn you.'

'*We*?'

But he'd rung off, and I was holding a dead receiver. I replaced it on its prongs and—strangely—Dorsey didn't sound as soothing any more.

*   *   *

When I'd arrived home I'd kidded myself that my next stop was going to be bed. Even after the guy who didn't want to part with his name had telephoned, I still toyed with the idea of Dreamland. Then I had second thoughts. I rang Rogate police station, warned them I had things to tell them about Service Areas on the M6, and laced my shoes on again. I tightened my tie, finished my coffee, then ducked into the weather and ploughed through the snow and into the car.

115

And now I was worried that Lyle might think I was pulling some sort of involved gag.

'Kay Mason?' he drawled.

'That was the name she gave me.'

'Why should she do that?'

'Do what?'

'Tell you her name?'

'For Christ's sake! I'd just saved her from being killed.'

'That's what *you* say.'

'Why else?'

'I can think of reasons,' he said pompously. He smiled. 'A whole raft of reasons, if you insist.'

'Why else should I drive her from one Service Area to another?'

He was keeping something to himself, and it was worrying. Inside, I was tending to panic a little.

I said, 'One Service Area to another. Why else should I pick her up?'

'Other reasons have been known,' he said teasingly. 'She was quite good-looking.'

'Smart,' I agreed. 'But what's that—'

'Oh, come *on*!' he mocked. 'Birds and bees. Little black bags. Or do you still believe in gooseberry bushes?'

I gaped a little, then said, 'She wasn't a pick-up, if that's what you're suggesting.'

'That's exactly what I'm suggesting.' He nodded.

'On a motorway?'

'There are junctions.'

'Eh?'

'Then side-roads ... then back to the motorway.'

'Look, if you think—'

'There are even other Service Areas, with conveniently shaded corners.'

'Of all the—'

'Don't play it *too* innocently, Thompson. Don't try *too* many haloes for size.'

'It didn't happen that way. That *wasn't* what happened.' And, maybe there was a touch of desperation in my voice. Slowly, and very deliberately, I said, 'She dodged the car. She slipped. She broke her hand.'

I willed him to believe me and, of course, he believed me. He didn't speak. He watched my face for a few drawn-out seconds. He just sat there and watched, without even the hint of an expression on his features. It was very disconcerting—and he knew it.

I tried to stare back, but muffed it. I could only notice that what I'd taken for a fancy shirt was, in fact, a particularly jazzy pyjama jacket, worn under his coat, with a silk scarf worn cravat fashion at the neck. The chances were that he was wearing pyjama bottoms under his trousers. He looked like a GP called out in the small hours.

Somehow it made him seem more human.

That, on the credit side. On the debit side, the office was cold. It was the cold peculiar to that created by a central heating system which has been switched off for some hours and no longer has muscle enough to counter a touch of frost riding the night air.

I blew out my cheeks, gave a quick shiver and said, 'It's not too warm in here.'

'She broke her hand.'

Lyle's voice had a faraway quality. It was soft, and he seemed to be speaking to himself, rather than to me.

He said, 'At the Service Area south of junction thirty-three—at the Forton Service Area—you performed minor first aid.'

'I've been trying to—'

'That, I believe.'

'Good of you.'

'The counter staff tell us they remember you asking for bandages.'

'And if you go to the other Service Area— the one south of junction twelve—'

'Junction eleven.'

'Eh?'

'You can't count, Thompson. It was junction eleven.'

'Oh!'

'Hilton Park Service Area. Where you were, earlier today.'

'They all look alike. But if you go there. If you ask there. They'll tell you—'

'Thompson.' He seemed to reach a decision. He leaned forward across the desk. He placed his forearms carefully on the surface and

118

steepled his index fingers. He spoke quietly, and a little intensely. He said, 'The Taske Force.'

I blinked.

'You know what I'm talking about?' he enquired.

'A London gang,' I offered. 'I see they're in today's headlines again. As I read things, they're trying to carve up The Smoke. I think they're pushing their luck. They're riding for a big fall.'

'No.' He shook his head. Slowly. Sadly. In a distinctly morose voice he said, 'What do you know about criminal gangs, Thompson?'

'The Kray twins,' I volunteered.

'Ah, yes. Reginald and Ronald. To say nothing of Charles.'

'The Richardsons.'

'Charlie and Eddie. The so-called "Torturers". The Glasgow razor gangs. The Messina brothers and their brothels. The race gangs. They come. They go.' He enjoyed a very melodramatic sigh. 'The Met,' he continued. 'They count their officers in thousands where we, in the provinces, count in hundreds. And their job—their main job—is to keep some sort of a check on mob violence. Murder. Feuding. Protection rackets. Dope rings. You name it—if it's rotten the Met collect it. But they keep the lid on—*just*! Most of the time the brew simmers and boils a little. But now and again it explodes. In the sixties it was the Krays and the

119

Richardsons. Today it's the Taske boys and the Haslop mob.' He paused, then ended, 'That's what you've grabbed a fistful of, Thompson.'

I blinked. I stared. I moistened my lips. Quite suddenly, I felt queasy. Almost physically sick. I swallowed, and tried to quieten my squirming guts.

'The woman,' he said quietly.

'Kay Mason?'

'Her name is Moira Taske.'

'No. It's Kay—'

'Moira Taske. Wife of Edward—Eddie— Taske. Sister-in-law to Henry—Harry— Taske. Her name is *not* Kay Mason. It never *was*.'

'Look,' I protested. 'When Cullpepper interviewed me, he was—'

'Cullpepper,' he said, very deliberately, 'is remarkably short-plankish. He's thick. Uniquely so. For that obvious reason, Cullpepper doesn't know *everything*.'

'Oh!'

'Moira Taske.' He leaned sideways a little, opened a desk drawer, took out a slim folder, opened the folder, then slipped a black-and-white photograph across the desk towards me. 'Not,' he said, 'Kay Mason. Moira Taske.'

It was her all right. And if the photograph was of Moira Taske, the woman I'd met up with wasn't called 'Kay Mason'.

'In the normal course of events,' he sighed,

'we would tell you to crawl back into your personal knot-hole and mind your own damn business. But, unfortunately, the events are *not* normal. And you're a private detective. You're an ex-investigative journalist. You have a long nose for these things, and I have to make a very important decision.'

He returned the photograph to its folder, returned the folder to its drawer, then said, 'The Taske brothers.'

'They're hitting the headlines,' I murmured.

'Quite.' He nodded. 'Eddie and Harry. The "Taske Force", as they like to be called. The Taske *gang*. How big?' He sucked his teeth, and continued, 'We-ell, they claim to be able to put more than two hundred "soldiers" on the streets, if necessary. But that includes members of various lesser, affiliated gangs. But they're big. That can't be denied. They're making news every day, these days. They're getting very brave. Hopefully, a little *too* brave.

'That, we know. That, the Met knows— specifically, the Flying Squad. That she drove north, in that Porsche of hers. Moira Taske. Eddie Taske's wife. That it took five Q cars— plus a van—to keep tabs on her. The squad boys were waiting at the Service Area exit. But you planted your size-tens on the nice, new, wet concrete and screwed everything rotten.'

He paused. His expression gave nothing away. He found cigarettes and lighter, held the open packet towards me, then thumbed the lighter and held the flame to each cigarette in turn.

He said, 'You read the tabloids?'

'Of course.'

'How the "Taske Force" and the Moody Gang—Joe Moody and his cousin "Big Bill" Haslop—are fighting for territorial rights. Trying to do a Kray/Richardson carve-up of the capital.'

'They're trying very hard,' I agreed.

'And beyond. Liverpool, Newcastle, Manchester. Every damn police force south of the border is girding its individual loins, ready to go to war. For myself...' He drew on the cigarette, then repeated, 'For me, they could all kill each other. The sooner the better. The world would be a cleaner place. And safer. But, of late, they're not just killing themselves. They're killing people who aren't in either gang.' He gave a quick, twisted smile and inhaled cigarette smoke again. He went on, 'Not particularly *nice* people. That, I grant you. In fact, rather disgusting—disagreeable—people. People who, for various reasons, won't "conform" to either gang's rule of behaviour.'

'It's common knowledge.' I waved my own cigarette around a little, to emphasise how blasé I was. 'Open any of the popular newspapers. It's there, on the front—'

'Not what *I'm* going to tell you,' he interrupted. 'You won't read anything about Moira Taske on Page Three. She was coming

122

north to do something. To see somebody. We'll never know what—or who. Just that she was ready to tell all the Tales of Arcady about her husband and his friends. So just listen, Thompson. Then keep your mouth tightly shut.'

I waited. I stayed silent. I had this creepy feeling; that something was coming, and that that 'something' was going to widen my eyes and stop my breath.

I still played at being unshockable.

I glanced at the radiator and murmured, 'The heating's off.'

'It is,' he agreed.

'I can stand shocks a lot better when I'm warm.'

He almost snarled, 'Thompson, you're not setting up home here. Don't get too carried away with the idea of shared confidentiality. You're being told things for a purpose. In the hope that you'll have enough simple gumption to keep out of everybody's way.'

'I get the general drift.'

'Good. Because I might as well tell you for starters: Moira Taske is dead. At a guess—and other than her murderer—you were about the last person to see her alive.'

'Her...' I swallowed. 'Her murderer?'

'You don't honestly think Taske was going to let her shoot off her mouth, do you?'

'I...' Again, I tried to relieve my dry throat. Then, 'She was—y'know ... she was his *wife*.'

'And husbands don't kill wives?' he asked sardonically.

'Yes, of course they do. But—'

'Of course they do,' he echoed sarcastically. He drew on his smouldering cigarette, then continued, 'We've mentioned the Kray brothers. Frances—Reggie's wife—drugged herself to death. She committed suicide because of the animal she'd married. Don't ask me why they hitch up in the first place. Some sort of fascination with living dangerously.'

'And—and Moira Taske—the woman I gave a lift to the other night—is *dead?* Murdered?'

'Specifically, hanged from a tree, in a coppice, not far from a village called Abbeystead. And *that's* only a couple of miles from the Service Area where you bandaged her hand.'

'I know where Abbeystead is,' I muttered.

'Her tongue was cut out, before they hanged her.'

I suddenly felt physically sick. I deliberately closed my eyes in an attempt to hang on to sanity. I took deep breaths and, when I was half-way composed, I reached across, without invitation, and helped myself to a cigarette from the packet which was still on the desk top. Lyle offered the flame of the lighter and allowed me a few moments in order to steady a violently rocking boat.

'Tough,' he said at last. 'But you had to

124

know. You were too involved not to be told.'

'She was—she was going to see someone?' I stammered.

'Somebody she could trust. Too many Met officers take a rake-off from the villains. They'll deny it, but it's true. Maybe she found a copper up north she could trust. Maybe anything. We'll never know.'

'When—er—y'know ... when did they find her?'

I asked the question merely as a stop-gap to my own racing thoughts. What Lyle was saying was still hammering in my brain. I had yet to come to terms with a particularly nasty piece of reality.

'Last night,' he said. 'Kids hunting around in the wood. The coppice. They found her. One of them's still in hospital recovering from the shock.'

'That I can believe. If her tongue was...' But I couldn't quite finish the sentence.

'A warning,' growled Lyle. 'Nobody tells tales on Taske and lives. The medics figure she was killed within a couple of hours—maybe a little more—of her last being seen at the Forton Service Area.'

'Jesus!' I breathed.

'You didn't kill her,' said Lyle gruffly. 'We've checked you out, obviously. You're in the clear, Thompson. Now, if you're wise, forget it. Be glad you're lucky. You could have been up to the eyes in fertiliser.'

*   *   *

I'd been a worried man driving to the police station. I was even more worried as I drove back to the flat above *The Wine Bibber*.

Moira Taske—Kay Mason—what the hell she was, and what the hell she'd been—had been property with a temperature far in excess of what I was used to handling. Before I'd turned private eye I'd grubbed around in various journalistic snake pits and, that being the case, I was not about to dismiss as high-flown hooey anything that Lyle had said.

Lyle was not one of those haystalk-in-the-ear, roll-on-Pension-Day provincial coppers who rock back on their heels, sway gently in the prevailing breeze and mouth sweet pontifications at the local Masonic Lodge. I'd watched Lyle at work in the past and knew that when Lyle said we were tangling with ogres, we were, indeed, tangling with ogres.

He'd explained (as if it had needed explanation) that the snouts handled by the Flying Squad did not provide make-believe griff. The squad boys paid only for the truth—or else! Therefore, when they said the Taske woman was travelling north to spill her guts to some gook she trusted, that was exactly what she'd been about on the motorway.

'Between London and Morecambe,' Lyle had explained. 'Maybe a copper. Maybe not a copper. Maybe *at* Morecambe. Maybe *before*

Morecambe. Maybe *after* Morecambe. The finer details aren't known.'

'Maybe at a motorway Service Area,' I'd growled.

'That is not impossible.'

'Therefore...'

'Therefore, whoever was out to stop the meeting might even toy with the idea that it's too late.'

'That *I'm* the guy she was going to spill her guts to.'

'Stranger mistakes have been made.' He seemed to find the possibility ever so slightly amusing. I'd suspected a distinct gleam in his eyes as he'd added, 'Of course, *we* know you're not.'

'The Flying Squad!' I'd done nothing to hide my disgust. 'Q cars, hot-shot tips from reliable snouts. And, at the end of it all, one almighty cock-up.'

'The squad boys were waiting.' He'd shrugged his shoulders slightly. 'Out there, by the pumps. Alongside the Service Area exit. But they were waiting for a red Porsche. Whereas yours is only...'

'A blue Ford,' I'd grunted.

'Not even the right colour.'

'And from here?' I'd asked.

'Your guess. My guess.' He hadn't quite chuckled but, given the ghost of an opportunity, and without the shadow of a killing hanging over the conversation, I'd been left in no doubt that it would have been there. He seemed to have seen something strangely amusing in the situation. Me? I saw nothing at all amusing in it.

We weren't even on a mutual level of humour.

*   *   *

And now it was past midnight—past the first hour of a new day—and the snow was easing a little (or maybe I was getting a little more used to it) and I parked the car outside the front of *The Wine Bibber*, locked it and, once more, trudged my weary way across the few yards separating me from my own doorstep. I seemed to have developed the habit of keeping ridiculously late hours.

The telephone bell started to ring as I climbed the stairs.

I picked up the receiver, grunted the number and was made even more worried by the smooth voice which came over the line.

'You are a foolish man, Mr Thompson.'

There was that slight pause, followed by tiny clicks before he spoke. He was ringing from a kiosk.

'Who's that?' I asked.

'Know merely that *I* know.'

'Eh?'

'And that you're a foolish man.'

'And you,' I snarled, 'are a prolonged pain in

the arse.'

'Going to the police.'

'How the hell do *you* know I've...'

'Everything, Mr Thompson. You can't do *anything* we don't know about.'

I dropped the receiver back onto its rest, ran from the room, raced down the stairs and hared into the street. I was going much too fast for the conditions. My feet skidded and I landed heavily on my left shoulder. It didn't matter. I'd seen all I wanted to see.

The telephone kiosk was about fifty yards away, out of line of my windows, but with a clear view of my front door. The man was moving out and hurrying down a side street.

I hoiked myself upright and, holding my shoulder, hurried as fast as I was able to the mouth of the side street. I saw the footprints in the snow. They led from the kiosk to a set of tyre marks. I saw the tail-lights disappearing in a cloud of exhaust fumes at the other end of the street.

Very slowly and very painfully I returned home. I'd lost the bastard, but it was nice to know I'd been right.

*   *   *

Had I been one of the present crop of fictional hard-nosed dicks—either private or official—I would have been up and about with the lark next morning, making every pair of shaky twos add up to an immaculate four. I would have allowed ice-cold needle jets to play upon my sun-bronzed body before slipping into custom-made shoes and expensive clothes, prior to wandering forth to do battle with the ungodly.

Unfortunately, I was for real!

I was Harry Thompson and Marks and Sparks provided most of what I wore.

I had a shower, but not until late morning because, until then, the water wasn't hot enough for real comfort and, anyway, I wasn't too sure who the ungodly were.

I was also in some pain.

Having slept until well past ten, I performed what ablutions I considered necessary, eased my way into shirt and trousers, then rang for a taxi to take me to Rogate-on-Sands Cottage Hospital. I was chock-a-block with sitting behind a steering wheel, and the pain from my shoulder gave possible promise of a prolonged stay, what with X-rays and what have you.

My own medic was on duty, it being his turn to check temperatures and take blood pressures. He was unkind enough to guffaw at the suggestion of broken bones.

'Sprained, old lad. Sprained, that's all. Take more water with it next time, eh?'

Thus the considered opinion and the bedside manner of one of the NHS's lesser luminaries. He prescribed glorified aspirins and sent me on my way.

Back at home I showered again, then dressed

more carefully before spending the rest of the afternoon nursing a slightly aching shoulder, enjoying spasmodic bouts of light reading and listening to tapes of Basie, Artie Shaw and Stan Kenton.

And, of course, thinking. This, the subconscious gluing together of half-formed ideas—which often gives better results than the deliberate under-the-skull meditations.

Meanwhile I reached certain conclusions. That this 'private investigator' way of earning a crust had its advantages. For sure I was never likely to get too rich. But as long as I kept my nose bright and shiny, as far as the police were concerned, life could be very interesting, if at times a little spooky.

Strange and good-looking women share your car on long motorway drives. Then when they leave your protective company they are murdered. Oddball clowns go out of their way to be over-mysterious and shoot stupid 'or else' spiels along telephone wires. You are hit in the face with sides of motor cars. You are hit on the shoulder by pavements. Whatever else, life is never boring.

By early evening I was hungry. The shoulder had rested itself into a dull but easily forgettable discomfort. I had a nice slice of legitimately earned loot from the illegal bacon caper. I decided that I owed Liz a decent meal.

I rang her and suggested *The Wine Bibber*.

'You won't have far to walk.' In the

131

background I heard the sound of something knocked sideways by one of the present-day, less-tuneful composers. She asked, 'What time?'

'Seven ... ish. That okay?'

'I'll be along.'

'Good.'

'Your treat?'

'My treat. I'll tell Bull to serve the best the house can offer, at about half-seven.'

'Something slightly more exotic than beans on toast right?'

She wasn't in a particularly pleasant mood. That was okay. I slammed the mood back at her.

I snapped, 'Let's say something slightly more tasteful than the cacaphonic mush you are, at this moment, listening to.'

'Harry, my love, you have no taste.'

'I married *you*.'

'Maybe my taste slipped for a moment.'

'See you at seven.'

'I'll be there.'

From which it might be deduced that we were not too crazy about each other, and that would be a very wrong deduction. Liz was all female, but she also had the ability to give and exchange minor insults, much as men do; men who enjoy a companionship far deeper—far closer—than the 'best friend' crap claimed by most women. It was part of her uniqueness. It was why, and however different our taste in

132

unimportant things, I could never divorce her, or even contemplate not seeing her with a steady regularity.

* * *

Bull had done us proud. I'd warned him about Liz's possible mood and he'd had a word with the gem of a chef he'd recently taken on. She, in turn, had presented a feast. King prawn cocktail for starters. Then fillet steak, with a choice of five fresh vegetables. We neither of us went for sweet but instead had port-fed Stilton, biscuits and Viennese coffee. All this with a Beaujolais chosen by Bull himself.

And, as we slowly worked our way through the feast, we talked. We exchanged ideas and opinions about the subject uppermost in our thoughts.

'She must have known what he was when she married him.'

Liz was very down to earth about such matters.

'You knew what I was,' I murmured.

'Straight. A fool, sometimes, but not bent.'

The table was tucked away in an alcove. There were four such alcoves, reserved for special occasions. They gave privacy, but they also gave a moderately unrestricted view of the main dining area and, beyond the dividing rail, the equally cosy drinking area. It was, I solemnly decided, one of the friendliest and

133

neatest eating-spots-cum-watering-holes I'd ever known.

Liz was saying, 'Too many junctions. Even too many Service Areas.'

'What?' I couldn't follow her thought process.

'I don't give a damn how big the gang is.'

'Oh, you mean the Taske Force crowd.'

'Not *that* big a crowd. You'd need a young army.'

Bull had wandered over to the table a couple of times to check that things were going smoothly. Almost an hour ago I'd spotted Lyle standing at the tiny bar, enjoying a glass of what I took to be his usual cider.

The snow had stopped.

When I'd come from the flat and waited for Liz in the foyer of *The Wine Bibber*, the strengthening frost had had that hard, brittle bite that brings on a feeling of slight panic at the possibility that the car might not have sufficient anti-freeze in its system. Nor had the town's gritters and ploughs made much of an impression away from the prom. Rogate-on-Sands, you must understand, is a seaside town. More than that, it is a summer holidaying town. The prom and its immediate environs take precedence over all else and, anyway, winter, snow, fog and ice—nobody is ever likely to be stranded at Rogate-on-Sands, the only fact worthy of consideration by the elders of the council.

But that is one reason why the car, out in the street, skidded. It was being driven too fast for the weather conditions and that too cannot be doubted. Equally, in leaving my car parked by the kerb outside *The Wine Bibber*, I too contributed to what happened.

We heard the car approaching. Some seem to doubt this, but I am absolutely sure. I heard the rev of the engine growing louder. Not the skid; tyres sliding on hard-packed snow make very little noise. But, for sure, I heard the car, immediately before the explosion.

Strangely, I did not 'hear' the explosion.

I *felt* it!

My seat was with its back to the window. I felt the savage push of the explosion; the flying glass spinning past my face and the shards burying themselves into Liz's cheeks, forehead and mouth; the masonry, the brickwork, the plaster and the woodwork which seemed to first lift, then smash into my spine and the back of my head.

For one moment, there was pain. Mad, impossible pain. Pain of such intensity that it held the chest in a grip tight enough to prevent breathing. Then, like the flicking of a switch, the pain vanished. I glimpsed the swirling fog of powdered debris and tried to stand up, in order to help Liz.

I placed my hands on the edge of the shattered table, urged myself to climb to my feet ... then passed out.

135

*　　　*　　　*

I returned to reality about two hours later, in the bed of a tiny side-ward in the Cottage Hospital. Somebody had been busy. I'd been stripped to the skin and was now wearing freshly laundered pyjamas.

I stared upwards and through the hole in the haze, Bull's face, then the face of a woman, wearing a nurse's cap floated into view.

I muttered, 'Liz? How's ...' as I tried to hoist myself into an upright position.

Bull's hands on my shoulders pushed me back onto the pillow, and he said, 'She's all right, son. Superficial ... that's all. She's down the corridor. Not yet quite out of Dreamland. But she'll be okay. You have my word. Just a modicum of luck and she won't even have a mark to show what happened.'

The knock-out potion took over again and I sank back into sleep and surfaced again just after midnight. An understanding nurse visited me and, very gingerly, helped me from my bed and half-carried me down the corridor to see Liz for myself. She was asleep, and her face looked not unlike a tightly stitched patchwork quilt, but the cuts were razor-thin and, with a calm sea and a following breeze, there'd be no disfigurement. I stayed in Liz's room until dawn. I sat on a chair by her bed and watched her sleep; it was the healthy sleep of exhaustion, and not the sleep of the anaesthetic. Until the sky lightened in the east, I sat there and held her hand.

At dawn, the nurse helped me back to my own side-ward and by that time I'd come up with a few answers.

*   *   *

Lyle visited on my second day of hospitalisation. He came at mid-afternoon, and he made it very obvious that it was an official visit and had little to do with my health.

Probably because of who he was, and what he was, the hospital authorities came up with some decent tea and some slices of sponge cake.

'Not bad food,' he observed.

'You should come more often. Until now the taste and standard has been slightly more nauseating than prison slop.'

He made-believe not to hear, took another bite of sponge cake, then said, 'We're still making enquiries, of course.'

'Enquiries?' If my stare bordered upon a glare, who could blame me?

'About the explosion. About the "why". About the "who".'

'The "why",' I snapped, 'is because they think somebody knows too much. The "who" is the Taske crowd.'

'Your motor car. Therefore *you're* the "somebody".'

I grunted some sort of an agreement.

He said, 'It was an electrical detonator. Simple but effective, obviously. The free-running, metal-ball type of connection.'

'Nice to know,' I sneered.

'If you'd been in the car. If you'd driven off—'

'I get the general idea.'

He sipped at the tea, and asked, '*Do* you know anything?'

'Nothing worth killing for,' I lied.

'Y'know what, Thompson?' He cocked his head to one side a little as he spoke. 'As far as the police are concerned, you're rapidly becoming a distinct pain in the arse.'

'That, too, makes me happy,' I murmured.

'What the hell do you *know*?' he asked. Then, 'What the hell do they *think* you know?'

'The two bastards who tried to kill the Taske woman at the Service Area,' I suggested. 'I saw them. Just a glimpse. No more than that, but in a line-up, memories can be jogged. One with whiskers. One clean-shaven.'

We sat in silence for a while. It was not a particularly awkward silence. More of a contemplatory silence.

He lighted a cigarette. Then he seemed to notice that I wasn't smoking, took the freshly lighted cigarette from his lips and held it towards me. I grunted thanks and took the proffered peace offering. Then he fished a second cigarette from its packet and lighted it.

We were (it seemed) like lovers. Like Paul Henreid and Bette Davis, lighting cigarettes for each other. We were like a re-run of *Now Voyager*—and, any minute, one of us would start the moon-and-stars spiel.

I waited, but he said nothing. He seemed to be waiting for me to make the first move.

He watched me, and smoked his cigarette, but didn't speak.

I said, 'You weren't there, Lyle. I *was*. They wanted her dead—whoever "they" were. They wanted her dead, and she *knew* they wanted her dead. She was scared, and with good cause. Dammit, *she* knew who they were. She as good as admitted that fact.'

'She knew before she died.'

'And now they're after me.'

'It follows.'

'Not just me. Liz, if she happens to be in the way. I tell you—'

'No. Let me tell you.' The worry was there, in the tone and in the facial expression. He pulled a heavy glass ash-tray on the side table a little nearer, then told his story, without interruption.

'It happened about twenty years ago, give or take a year. I'd just moved into CID. Detective Constable. Word came up from the Met. Hints, then verification. Verification—the full story—after the dust had settled.

'This tearaway, who was making a name for himself in the Elephant and Castle area. He'd

139

collected a string of call girls. No slags. High class tail, and expensive. He was also getting some sort of mob organised. Moving into Protection. The usual thing.

'Anyway, one of the call-girl team was special. Must have been. The hoodlum fell for her. Pulled her out of the game and set her up in a luxury flat in the St John's Wood district.

'Then,' he paused, knocked ash from his cigarette into the ash-tray, then continued, 'he married her. Rumour has it that, for a few years, she had an influence on him. A good influence. Not the prozzie with a heart of gold. Not that ancient fairy tale. Just that he seemed less of an animal than before.'

He stopped talking for a few seconds. He gave the impression that he expected me to respond, but I stayed dumb.

'One of your crowd screwed it up,' he continued.

'A private detective?' I asked innocently.

'A reporter. A newspaper man.'

'Oh!'

'He tried a Casanova on the wife, and she responded. They had quite a thing going for themselves for a few months. Then the hoodlum found out.' Without a change of tone, Lyle went on. 'He brought the wife and the newspaper man to face each other. Blew the man's brains out, then tied the woman's wrists together, hung her up on a meat hook, then got to work with a stock-whip.' There was a final

140

pause, then he ended, 'Taske, of course. I'm told she still had the whip-scars across her back. When they cut her down ... that's what you're up against Thompson. I thought you should know.'

'And now,' I said, 'he has his sights on *me*.' I tried to sound worried. It wasn't difficult. I *was* worried.

'You had to be told.'

I took a final pull on my cigarette, then squashed it out in the ash-tray.

In as calm a voice as possible I said, 'He's out to kill me ... unless I kill him first. If I do that, can you guarantee to keep him away from Liz?'

*   *   *

I had underestimated Lyle. He had depths I had not yet plumbed. He hadn't even blinked at my suggestion. He'd merely murmured, 'Naturally,' as if what I'd said hadn't needed to be said. As if it had been in no way unexpected.

I gave myself time to walk to the window, turned, rested my rump on the radiator and said, 'What do you intend doing? To keep Liz safe, I mean.'

'The force has a Tactical Firearms Unit.'

'And?'

'We try to be modern. Sex equality, that sort of thing. Two of the members of the unit are policewomen.'

'They can't live with her, night and day.'

141

'For a limited time,' he argued. 'Those two, and a couple of male members of the unit. For—say—a month? If you haven't done what you intend doing by then, you won't have much chance.'

'You'll look after her?' I made it into a question, and the urgency of the question got through to him.

'Someone else will die before she does,' he promised. Then, 'You belong to a gun club. I'll leave the choice of handguns to you. I'll do all *I* can. No questions—within limits, of course.'

'You can *do* that?' I think my surprise showed itself.

'Thompson.' His lips bowed into a quick, tight smile. 'We take an oath when we join. Within the limits of the law, we keep that oath. But for *some* of us ... if it's a straight choice between the oath and the law, we make that choice. Sometimes we come unstuck. Sometimes we even end up in prison—being sued for Wrongful Arrest, Wrongful Imprisonment ... but we rarely *are* wrong. It's one of the hidden risks every good copper has to take.'

'Oh!'

'Not for *you*.' The impression was that he was backing down. That he was already regretting what he'd said and how far he'd gone. He growled, 'You can boil away in your own hot water for all I care.'

'Well, thank you, kind sir.'

'Just that Taske and his crowd have made monkeys of the force—even the Met—for too long.'

'That's what I thought,' I smiled.

'And, anyway, I'd hate anything to happen to Liz.'

'So would I,' I assured him. 'So would I.'

*   *   *

Two days later, I discharged myself. Maybe the quack was right. Maybe a couple more days in the hospital wouldn't have come amiss. On the other hand, maybe the medic was playing it safe. I, personally, didn't give much of a damn. I had things to do, and the things I had to do wouldn't keep.

First of all I needed money, and my cheque-book had been in my breast pocket when the bang had caved in the front of *The Wine Bibber*. A quick call at my branch of Nat West sorted that problem out, then I walked around a few corners to where I'd once lived. It must have been quite an explosion. The front of Bull's place had been pushed in, which meant that *my* homely little nest was minus a wall and open to the elements. The floor was on a slant, and seemed to be in danger of slipping into the street. Exposed as it was, the wallpaper looked cheap and ugly. Somehow, the divan had wedged itself drunkenly into a corner of the chimney jamb.

143

The builders were already at work. A trio of labourers were carefully shifting the rubble, one brick at a time.

I ducked under the scaffolding doing double-duty as a barrier to inquisitive pedestrians and holding some of the fabric of the building in place.

One of the labourers shouted, 'Watch it, mate!'

'I live here,' I said sourly. Then corrected it to 'I *lived* here.'

'Lucky old you.'

I looked for a few more moments, but I did not linger. A gutted building is a sorrowful sight. It has its own personal ugliness. It is an uncomfortable, nervous place. It seems to have lost far more than its privacy and shows a shameful and embarrassing exposure.

I walked the streets until I came to Bull's son-in-law's house. Bull was out. His daughter explained.

'He's with the insurance assessor. He was wise. He over-insured.' She smiled and added, 'You'll have a nice place to live in in about three months, Mr Thompson.'

'Will he be in this evening?' I asked. I didn't feel like pressing the 'nice new place' angle.

'Oh, yes. We've a meal at about five-thirty. He'll be home by then.'

'I'll see him about seven. Okay?'

I left, and went for a light meal.

For a man straight from a hospital bed, I was

144

quietly knackering myself. I'd never felt as tired before in my life.

I pulled myself together, then wandered along to the garage I'd always used to service my cars. I told the man what I wanted and asked him to come up with some ideas.

'An Escort XR3,' he suggested. He led me across the showroom to a black Ford, with tinted windows and a sun-roof. He said, 'Less than ten-thousand on the clock. Five-speed gearbox. Automatic choke. Electronic ignition.'

'Plus,' I grunted, 'one arm and one leg.'

'We can reach a deal,' he assured me. 'Get behind the wheel. Try it for size. Then we'll take it for a trial spin.'

It was a nice car. Out on the motorway it stretched itself and gave promise of three-figure speeds if they were ever needed. Nor was the price in telephone numbers. Its only previous owner had gone bankrupt and been flushed down the tube.

'Can I drive it away?' I asked.

'Let me check with your insurance certificate. If that's okay, you needn't bother getting from behind the wheel.'

It wasn't quite as easy as that but, within the hour, I was driving the car from the forecourt, with a full tank of juice.

I drove north along the coast and ended up at Lytham St Annes. I bought myself a toothbrush, toothpaste and pyjamas, then booked in at the Clifton Arms Hotel and made believe I could afford their brand of luxury. In the en-suite bathroom I soaked the weariness from my limbs before taking the lift down to the restaurant, booking a late dinner, then returning to the car and heading south for a return to Rogate-on-Sands and my meeting with Bull.

*　　　*　　　*

Bull said, 'It's not fair, not to tell Liz.'

I was, I thought, guarding my back by telling Bull. He was interested enough to try to dissuade me but, when he couldn't, he insisted I let Liz in on my knowledge.

'Liz and Lyle,' he pressed.

'The hell with *that*. Too many in the know and the whole pantomime folds.'

'You're going to tell *Taske*,' he argued.

'Eventually. When I have him firmly by the balls.'

We were in his heated greenhouse. Just the two of us. It was a very moderately-sized greenhouse and the forty-watt bulb fixed in the apex of the roof turned the panes into black mirrors, reflecting us a score of times at a dozen angles. It was a tiny, cosy, womb-like place of our own.

He repositioned a label in one of the seed trays a fraction of an inch and said, 'It's a different world, Harry. A dangerous world.'

146

'They're mortal,' I grunted. 'Sub-human, but mortal.'

'Tell Lyle,' he begged. 'If he backs you—and you say he does, even unofficially—he'll take some of the pressure off.'

'I'm the one that's putting on the pressure.'

'Please!' His reflection stared back at me beseechingly. 'Don't say I said so—but *please* tell Lyle.'

*   *   *

I slept on it and, having reached certain conclusions, I breakfasted on kippers, toast and marmalade, then strolled through Lytham shopping centre until I came to a gent's outfitters where I bought the works, from the skin out. It was quality stuff and, being quality, it wasn't cheap. Then back to the hotel for a shower and the delight of new clothes.

And, after that, back south, towards Rogate-on-Sands, then inland to the 'Pull and Nor'.

Some men prefer football or golf. Some cricket. Some chess or bridge. Some gardening. Some photography. Me? For me it was target practice at my club, the Pullbury and Norton Rifle and Pistol Range. The 'Pull and Nor' is, without doubt, one of the best gun clubs in the North-West. Its ranges and galleries provide just about anything a gun nut could wish for.

I had my own handgun. A Walther P38

(strictly a P39 which, as any shootist knows, is a P38 manufactured specifically for the Swiss Army.). It weighed 1.84 lb. Its feed system carried an 8-round magazine, and it fired a 9 mm Parabellum shot at the rate of 30 rpm.

The law required that I kept the Walther under lock and key in the club's security room, but it was my weapon and I could handle it well. I also liked to fire on the range with one of the club's revolvers. The occasional few rounds with a pump-action shotgun also added spice to life.

In truth, I counted the 'Pull and Nor' as one of my life's indulgences.

At times, Liz argued and muttered silly remarks about phallic symbolism but, as I pointed out, it could equally be argued that she was indulging in a sub-conscious fantasy about 'muzzle velocity'.

We agreed to differ.

What Liz could never understand was the simple club-room side of things. It *was* a club. Primarily a club. There was a Ladies' Section, a Mixed Section and (the one I favoured) a Stag Section. We were the smallest section of the three but (we claimed) we included the best marksmen of the club in our number.

The Stag Section (like the Ladies' Section) had its own annex from the main club-room, and that was where I ended up. It was cosy. It had its own tiny, open fire, its own coffee machine and its own opening to the bar. It had deep armchairs, a scattering of side-tables and a selection of carefully chosen magazines with which to while away the time between shooting sessions.

I collected the Walther and ammunition from the security room, then spent about thirty minutes in the Stag Section annex.

I called on Joseph, the club steward, in his office and told a very convincing lie.

'The firing pin's out of alignment.' I held out the Walther for him to see the weapon. 'It needs a gunsmith before it's safe to fire.'

'Oh dear,' said Joseph. In truth, and despite his position, he knew as much about guns as he knew about microbiology. He opened a drawer of his desk and said, 'If you'll sign a disclaimer form, to keep everything above board.'

Ten minutes later I was driving back to Rogate with a semi-automatic pistol and ammunition in my pockets.

*   *   *

I stood at the end of the pier, gazed down over the waist-high railings at the foam-flecked waves of the incoming tide and wished to hell I'd had the simple gumption to say 'No' when the Taske woman had dived for safety. It wasn't my business. It had never *been* my business. What hooliganism the London villains indulged in had no place in *my* world.

I didn't want to kill anybody. Not now ...

not after that moment of savage hatred I'd felt when the shards hit Liz's face. That emotional temperature doesn't last. A normal person cools off and, although still angry, no longer wants to kill.

But Taske and his minions had gone too far. In effect they'd declared war on me. The woman might have talked. That she *hadn't* mattered not at all. The possibility was enough. Enough to try to kill me. Enough to try to kill Liz.

The rogues of the species. They enjoy their work—enjoy their villainy—and they enjoy their killing.

I stood there, and tried to understand the Taskes of this world. I tried to figure out what it was all about. All this blood and guts and general arsing around playing homicidal tag.

I figured it was maybe about ordinary people, living ordinary lives. Not wondering whether a bomb's going to explode in their face. A bullet take them in the back. Not being too scared to go out of their own front door. Not staying awake at nights, worrying about the next day.

That was what the Taskes of the world worked to destroy. Simple, ordinary living.

They collected large sums of tax-free loot for enjoying themselves.

And what enjoyment!

You wanted somebody knee-capped? You wanted somebody crippled? Somebody blown up? You wanted pain? Heartbreak? Maybe even simple terror? Fine. You paid a bastard like Taske, and he delivered.

I muttered, 'And now, given the ghost of a chance he'll kill *me*. If I don't kill *him* first. He'll kill Liz . . . because *his* old lady might have told me something, and I might have passed that something on to *my* old lady.' Maybe I chuckled. Maybe I didn't chuckle. As sure as hell I'd little to chuckle about. I murmured, 'Thompson, old pal, until now, you haven't been worth a quick piss into the wind. Now— thanks to your good manners—you're priceless.' I turned, slowly, and gazed at the promenade, beyond the pier head. At the flats and nursing homes. At the hotels. Good hotels, with flash interiors, comfortable beds and beautifully served meals. Hotels where the comparatively well-off stayed when on holiday. Where a degree of luxury ensured that Rogate-on-Sands attracted only a certain type of holidaymaker.

Slowly I walked from the pier end. My shoes made measured footfalls on the narrow oak plankings of the pier floor. Beneath me, amongst the iron stanchions and the upright piles, the incoming tide swirled and sucked. In the deserted pavilion—beyond an open exit door, ajar and with its crash-bar hanging loose—a lonely workman hammered in an echoing hall, with the tinny music of transistorised pop as a fitting accompaniment.

151

Another year meant another season. Within the next few months the population would double, and more than double. Before-breakfast strollers would nod and smile early-morning greetings to their own kind. Strangers would share promenade shelters and chat to each other as if to life-long friends. The chemist shops would have a great upsurge in the number of films handed in for developing. The cafes and tea shops would vastly increase their sales of cakes and pots of tea.

It was Rogate-on-Sands. It was so monumentally *innocent*. It was so different—so much *better*—than the foul set-up I found myself mixed up in.

Thus my thoughts as I left the pier and turned along the promenade.

Then a voice called, 'Excuse me!'

The prom was just about deserted and, for a moment, I didn't realise that the owner of the voice was trying to attract *my* attention.

Again the voice called, 'Excuse me! Thompson, isn't it?'

I turned and saw the middle-aged, well-dressed man sitting in the parked car, holding the door open and smiling in my direction.

'I'm sorry.' I didn't know him and I frowned puzzlement as I moved towards the car.

'It *is* Harry Thompson?'

'Yes.' I nodded. I looked down at the middle-aged man and said, 'Do I know you?'

'No.' The middle-aged man was still smiling.

It was a pleasant enough smile. A friendly smile. As he slipped the silencered pistol from the deep pocket of his jacket he continued, 'You don't know me. You never *will* know me. Neither of us have missed much.'

I was diving to my left as the first shot hissed past my right shoulder. The second shot gouged a mark in the concrete as I rolled away from the kerb. I don't know where the third shot went. I was too busy sprinting the few yards to the dubious cover given by stacked and tarpaulined deck-chairs.

I heard the car start and risked a peep along the top of the stacked chairs. It was leaving the scene remarkably unhurriedly. I visualised the middle-aged man carefully changing up the gears . . . still with the hint of a smile on his face.

*   *   *

I think bravado took me to Liz's place. Bravado, plus a growing sense of outraged fury at the realisation that a no-longer-young goon had been sent to finish me off.

I'd intended calling, prior to visiting Liz in hospital, to pick up any accumulated mail. Before I'd left the pier I'd decided to perform that small errand. But now I think I was using the collection of mail as an excuse.

I walked, for no better reason than that it was not too far and the night was cold, crisp and starless. It would freeze before morning;

that shiny, iron frost that sends the temperature plunging to zero and below. Right now it was cold, but not bitingly so, and the street lamps were lit and, with luck, I'd hear the early evening news on Liz's radio.

Her apartment was, in effect, a ground-floor flat. Purpose-built and with a degree of luxury. Much better than my place had been. A couple of streets inland from the coast, because she knew Rogate as well as I did. Her place wasn't sand-blasted every time the wind blew from the west. If necessary, the windows could be opened without a miniature gale blowing through the rooms.

And talking of windows...

One of them wasn't properly closed. The panes were a little skew-whiff to their companion windows in the reflection of the street lighting. The window had been opened, then not properly closed.

I knew my Liz. I knew her well enough to know that *her* windows would be fully closed against the weather. She'd left them to join me at *The Wine Bibber*. She wouldn't have left a ground-floor window unlocked, much less not quite closed.

I ducked under the window line and ended up at the door. I pushed at it, but it was closed. Very gently I turned the knob, but the door was locked. I took out my key, inserted it into the lock and, at the same time, eased the Walther from my mac pocket.

My entry into the apartment was silent, and almost in slow motion. Beyond the door, in the hall, I stood motionless and listened. From the lounge came the soft sound of cracking and sawing. I moved to the lounge door, put my hand round the jamb and switched on the light as I threw the door open.

The man was crouched at Liz's desk. By the light of a pencil torch he was trying to force the drawers with what looked like a flick-knife.

He was in his thirties—early thirties—with a few days growth of whiskers at his jowls. He was dark and long-haired. Of a gypsy appearance, and he gave an angry, snarling yell as he launched himself at me, the flick-knife reaching out for my throat.

I shot him.

I'd never shot a man before. I wasn't expecting what happened.

The whole of him—bones, flesh and muscle—seemed to turn to jelly. Instantly. His momentum carried him no more than two feet, then he was a shapeless bundle on the carpet. It was very disconcerting. I'd aimed for the shoulder, but I'd hit him in the upper chest. There was blood—bright red, arterial blood that left his chest in rhythmical spurts—and there was some gurgling as (I think) he tried to speak. But, most of all, there was blood. More blood than I imagined any human being could hold.

For a moment I was stunned into inactivity.

Then came the urge to pick up the telephone and dial triple-nine. I wanted the police, I wanted an ambulance. I wanted *anything*!

Then, with equal speed, came the realisation that I could have nothing.

The man was dead. As near dead as to make no difference. And, as if to underline that fact, he gave a final, prolonged gurgle, shot out his legs into a stiffened position, then heel-tapped the carpet in a macabre tattoo. Then he lay still. Without movement. Without sound.

No more blood. No more gurgling. He was dead ... nothing surer.

I left the room and closed the door. I left the apartment and closed the front door. Out in the street I discovered that my face was streaming with sweat.

*   *   *

There is much loose talk about 'select clubs'. The Houses of Parliament; The Mile High Club; White's; Pratt's.

You have my assurance. Of all the 'clubs' in the world, there is none more select than 'The Murderers' Club'. Ms Highsmith, Mr Le Carré, Ms Rendell, Mr Francis—and a whole bean-bag full of other story-tellers—claim to write their yarns around the crime of murder. They spin their fantasies, but it is on a par with a man who has never had a woman trying to explain the joys of love to a fellow-virgin.

156

Me? I had killed. I was still trembling. I had just paid my entrance fee to *the* 'select club' of all the 'select clubs' ... and, when the time came, the membership fee would include a lifetime behind granite walls.

I was sweating, but I was also unbelievably cold, and the cold had nothing to do with the weather. It had everything to do with blind panic and, for a moment, the panic almost won.

Then I took maybe half a dozen deep, deep breaths and, very gradually, my mind started to function.

The man I'd killed. Who the hell was he? One of Taske's henchmen? And, if from Taske, was he alone? Logic suggested he *was* a Taske 'soldier', but what on earth he was up to? Burgling Liz's place was beyond my comprehension. But if he *was* from Taske the chances were he wasn't alone.

I stepped into the gloom of a nearby doorway and looked up then down the street. Other than a youth on a bicycle, it was deserted.

Four cars were parked. They all looked empty. I tried to remember the make of car the smiling, middle-aged man had been driving, but couldn't.

I stood there for maybe five minutes. I tried to kid myself I was being crafty. I wasn't. I was scared, and hadn't quite worked out what to do next.

Then I moved nearer to the centre of the town. I zigzagged like a crazy man. I doubled back upon myself at least four times. At each corner I stopped, listened and waited. Eventually I almost convinced myself that anybody tailing would have either been lost or would have bumped into me.

I ducked into one of the main pubs and went straight to the Men's Room. I relieved myself, then washed my hands and stared at the white face and wild eyes of a frightened man. In the bar I tried to check that the number of customers was the same as it was when I'd entered. It was no good. I could only guess. I hurried from the pub via a side entrance. Then onto the front, and into one of the small hotels. I made for the dining-room, pretended to change my mind and ended up in the lounge. Instead of sitting down, I turned and again made for a side entrance. One or two people stared. I realised I was making something of an exhibition of myself.

Outside I walked, as normally as possible, towards the prom. Towards where I'd parked the Ford. I wanted out. I wanted away from this town where strange men tried to shoot me, where I'd been jockeyed into committing murder.

In the car I simply sat. I must have sat, eyeing every other car for half an hour. Watching and wondering. I sat there long enough to smoke two cigarettes. Then I turned the ignition key and drove north to Blackpool.

I knew Blackpool. I could lose *anything* in Blackpool. Anybody could. Ask the taxi drivers. North along the prom and there's half a dozen places where even a passable driver can make a swift U turn without sweat. Anybody following you isn't following you any more. I was satisfied. Unless somebody had cracked the 'invisibility' riddle I was on my own.

I made for Preston and the A6. Not the M6. The M6—any motorway—was going to put me into an elongated rat trap. Mile after mile of carriageway without a turn off. I had to remember the possibility—however remote— that I *might* have a tail on me. That I *might* have been picked up and that Taske was already organising something particularly nasty.

North of Preston I turned off for Scorton, found a kiosk and phoned Bull.

*   *   *

I'd said, 'Bull, just listen. Don't interrupt. Don't ask questions till I've finished. Just listen, very carefully and remember, this isn't a gag. None of it's a gag. So just *listen.*'

Then I'd taken a couple of deep breaths, tried to collect my thoughts, and started.

'There's a body in Liz's place. A man. A burglar. I called round there and disturbed him. He came for me with a knife, and I shot

159

him. I didn't *mean* to kill him. But I did. I don't know his name. I don't *know* him. I don't even know what he was after.

'But tell Lyle. Tell him not to make waves organising a murder enquiry. It was me. When this lot's finished, I'll give myself up.

'And if he looks on the prom—Lyle, I mean—if he looks on the prom. Near the pier head. He'll find a bullet scar on the tarmac. Some bastard shot at me. Three shots. One hit the ground. I think *he* was from Taske. But that's all I know.'

Bull growled, 'You've had a busy day, boy.'

'Yeah.'

'What next, Harry? Y'know—how much more punishment can you take?'

'I'm going to Warton Sound. Rex Kelly. He's the key to it. It was *him* she was making for.'

'You sound sure, boy.'

'I'm sure. Where else? Once I knew she was Taske's woman, the rest fell into place.'

'You have a gun, then?'

'Eh?'

'A gun. You say you think you shot somebody at Liz's place. You must have a gun?'

'My own. The Walther.'

'Oh!'

'And I don't *think* I shot somebody. I *know* I did. And that he's dead.'

'Harry.' It came over with a certain groaning

quality. 'Tell Lyle, eh? Give yourself up. Whatever. This Taske Force thing. It's too big. A hell of a lot too big for *us* to beat it.'

'*You* tell Lyle,' I insisted. 'And let Liz know. What I think about her. Tell her *that*, too. And stay near the phone, Bull. Please.'

'For Christ's sake, Harry. Don't—'

'That's all,' I cut in. 'I'm on my way to Warton Sound. I'll be in touch when I've seen Kelly.'

I hung up and returned to the car. I didn't wait. I *daredn't* wait. Bull was so right, and I was so wrong. Added to which, I was still scared witless.

*   *   *

Rex Kelly. Remember him? A few years back he 'disappeared', but up to that time he was as near a household name as any news photographer can get. That's the guy. Remember? That's the 'Rex Kelly' I'm on about.

Let me tell you about him.

He started to become known at about the time when I was doing the investigative stuff at full throttle. When I left the newspaper rat race, he was quite famous. He'd pulled various 'photographer of the year' awards. He could use a camera like Rembrandt used a brush. He was good enough to furnish a series of exhibitions—and rarely showed the same

161

picture twice. His photograph of circus tigers had the stench of the big cats about it. His shot of tractors bringing in the harvest was a poem of nature and steel working together. His photograph of a diesel train rounding a slight bend and disappearing into a foliage-fringed tunnel was (and still is) a sheer gem of implied pornography. When he was in full flow, the argument was about who was *second*-best.

And this was the guy who'd bedded Taske's wife, Moira. Not the poor goon who'd had his head blown off. Maybe him, *too*. But not *only* him.

In the old days, I'd met Kelly a few times at various Press World bashes. He'd always counted himself as a few miles higher than us slobs from the sticks, and the old Fleet Street crowd had paid due homage. Me, too, come to that. Whatever his mannerisms—however bad his manners nobody could take top spot away from him.

Then had come the Taske business. Word had filtered north. Stories. Gossip. No proof, of course. Only that Kelly had hit the high timber when Taske showed his teeth ... and that he'd stayed in the high timber, and allowed another man—a mere reporter—to pay the price of his pleasure.

A genius—that was Rex Kelly ... but not too nice a guy.

Lyle, then, had got the right scenario. He'd just confused a couple of characters.

For myself, I'd re-met Kelly about four years previously. Another minor get-together of news-carriers. At Morecambe, this time. And I'd been as tight as a tic, and I'd met another member of the fraternity, equally drunk. We'd been so damn drunk, in fact, that we'd talked slush to each other for almost half an hour before we'd recognised each other.

Kelly had crawled from under his stone in the hope of re-kindling something he'd once had. Meeting guys from a world he'd raced away from. A form of homesickness, I suppose. Not that he even hinted that he wanted to come back, not even when slewed. But for a few hours—even uninvited—he'd wanted to talk with his own kind.

In a boozed-up stupor Kelly had told me. He had this isolated bungalow, on the sea shore, at Warton Sound. And Warton Sound was so minuscule that it only existed on a few maps. North of Carnforth. South of Silverdale. West of Warton, and tucked away in a corner of Morecambe Bay.

It was where I was making for.

It was where Moira Taske had *been* making for—I was ready to bet my eyeballs on it!

*   *   *

That was where I was going. But first I spent the night in the car park of a pub off the A6.

It was cold. Too cold for anything more

substantial than a quick cat nap every hour or so. I was off, before dawn, with the heater on at full and the deserted road ahead of me showing verges white with hoar-frost.

I breakfasted at a greasy spoon on Morecambe front, then I visited a public convenience and had a wash and spruce up. Then a brisk walk along the prom to bring myself fully awake.

Morecambe...

It tries to be a polite sister to Blackpool. More cultured, more genteel, more well-behaved than Blackpool. But Blackpool is consciously and unashamedly vulgar; it talks of 'golden beaches' when, in fact, it means miles of sewage-rimmed sand; it boasts of 'beautiful parks and walk-ways' when, in fact, it presents little more than acre upon acre of concrete. Blackpool is coarse and common, ill-bred and rude. It is blue, unrefined and naughty. But it is loved—even glorified—because it does not even try to pretend to be what it is not. It is one great belly laugh, whereas Morecambe is a prolonged smirk.

People 'love' Blackpool, whereas people only 'like' Morecambe.

I reached the open-air swimming complex, turned and hurried back to the car. The north-westerly came in, from across the bay, with the edge of a razor.

I reached the car, climbed inside, then lighted a cigarette.

164

Quite suddenly I realised I was deliberately wasting time. I was still scared. The Walther—not a particularly heavy handgun—weighed heavily in my mac pocket. It was there for a purpose, and I had little doubt that, eventually, the purpose would be called for.

Meanwhile, I was a most reluctant gunman. I'd killed. The corpse sprawling on Liz's carpet was proof enough for that. I'd killed (I told myself) in self-defence. I myself had even been shot at. Both Liz and I had been the intended victims of a deliberately placed bomb. Luckily, we'd lived—but, only *luckily*.

Logic suggested that I should be stalking the streets, finger on trigger, homicidal intentions in mind. But that wasn't the case. Had I thought that things would have quietened down—that Liz, at least, would have been allowed to live in peace—I would have walked into the nearest police station, given myself up and risked a prison sentence for shooting the intruder who'd been forcing the desk.

But things were not likely to quieten down. Like it or lump it, I was at the deep end of a world where pain and bloodshed were the only legitimate coinage. Taske's world. And Taske had to be removed if that world was ever likely to end.

I threw what was left of the cigarette through the open window of the car, turned the ignition key and started my journey to Warton Sound.

*   *   *

The road was fine, north through Hest Bank, Bolton-le-Sands and Carnforth. Beyond Carnforth, however, the way led from the main road, along an unmarked track, across the railway line, and then petered out in the shallow slope of beach pebbles, shingle and driftwood debris.

I left the car and walked. Maybe a mile. Maybe a little more. There must have been a better way to reach the bungalow but, if so, it was from inland and, to reach it I'd have had to back-track far more than I was prepared to.

There was a small wood—a coppice—which covered no more than two acres and ended where the pebbles began. And the bungalow was tucked away under the trees, with an open view seaward and the gloom of the wood to its rear.

I was in a situation new to me. I didn't want to play Cowboys and Indians. It seemed reasonable to assume that Kelly had no reason to link me with Taske, much less Taske's wife. I made no attempt at not being seen. I climbed the shallow wooden steps leading to the verandah and pressed the door bell.

From above my head—from a small microphone-cum-loudspeaker—a voice asked, 'Who is it?'

I tilted my head, and said, 'Thompson. Harry Thompson.'

166

'Harry who?'

'Thompson. We met a few years ago, at one of the Northern journalist bashes.'

'Sorry. I don't know you.'

'Yes, you do. We were both drunk at the time. Morecambe.'

'No.'

'You gate-crashed. You said I had to call if I was ever near Warton Sound.'

'I don't know what you're talking about. I don't know you, whoever you are. Go away.'

I gave him a moment of silence then, very deliberately, I said, 'I could, of course, ask Taske to send somebody round.'

The pause before he asked, 'Who's Taske?' wasn't quite right. It was too short; as if just about long enough to catch his breath.

I said, 'He'll introduce himself when he arrives.'

'No!'

'No?' I asked.

'Are *you* from Taske?'

'No. I don't like him any more than you do.'

'In that case—'

'In that case,' I interrupted, 'let's get together and found a mutual I-Hate-Taske society.'

Another slice of silence slipped into the conversation. I heard a soft click; an electrically operated door lock being operated.

Kelly's voice said, 'Okay. The door's unlocked. You can come in.'

I stepped forward, turned the knob and pushed open the door.

There was the roar of an explosion from in front of me and, at the same time, there came a howl of pain and a bullet ploughed through ceiling plasterboard above my head. The gun clattered to the floor. Kelly nursed his wrist and sobbed with pain. I stepped smartly into the hall and picked up the gun. It was a .45 Colt magnum. As I emptied the cylinder of what rounds remained, I said, 'Throw it next time. You'll have a better chance of hitting something.'

'I've broken my wrist,' he sobbed.

'Quite possibly,' I agreed. 'This toy isn't meant to be fired one-handedly. You've been watching too many Westerns.'

I swung my arm and sent the bullets arcing away, to mix with the pebble and shingles. Then I dropped the revolver beyond the door and onto the floor of the verandah and slipped the Walther from my mac pocket.

Kelly shied away, still clutching his injured wrist.

'You *are*,' he croaked. 'You *are* from Taske.'

'Let's talk.' I back-heeled the door closed and motioned with the automatic. 'Let's stop the yes-you-are-no-I'm-not routine. Let's just sit and talk. Meanwhile you can hope you're wrong, and that I'm not lying.'

*   *   *

By noon we were walking back to the car. Across the shingle and the tide debris. Kelly had his wrist in a sling. It might, or might not, have been broken. It mattered not at all to me. He'd tried to shoot me and with a .45 magnum he would undoubtably have killed me. Such young cannons are not to be shrugged off with an airy laugh. But at least now he knew. Should some visitor from the Taske crowd call, he now knew what *not* to do.

Meanwhile, it must be admitted that I was strangely disappointed in Rex Kelly.

I wonder. What sort of a man was Constable? What sort of drinking buddy was Joseph Haydn? An evening with George Gershwin—and *without* a piano—a warm memory, or a pain in the neck? That's what I mean. Rex Kelly was (or, at least, had been) a giant in the journalistic world. Perspective, angle, filter, surround, contrast, light and shadow. He could handle these things like no other. For that reason he'd once been my paragon. But no more.

He was a slob. The only thing that interested him was his own miserable skin. No threats had been needed. No pressure. Merely the assurance that he would suffer no pain. That his fat and shiny carcass would not be damaged in any way.

We stumbled across the shingle and I asked, 'She *was* making for your place, of course?'

'Yeah. I suppose, so. The selfish cow.'

'Selfish!' I paused long enough to stare my near disbelief. 'You,' I said, 'let another man get murdered for *your* billy-goating.'

'I couldn't stop it.' Then, 'And, anyway, she insisted that I keep my head down.'

'I doubt if you took much encouraging.'

'What good would it have done. Two of us dead.'

'She contacted you, right? Within the last few days?'

'Of course. She phoned.'

'And?'

'She wasn't too specific. But she's always wanted the pictures.'

'I don't blame her. I don't blame her at all.'

The soles of our shoes made slow hissing noises as we ploughed across the tiny pebbles and broken shells of the shingle. It wasn't much easier than walking through soft sand.

Out by the shoreline dippers and waders formed a million tiny, shimmering dots. Gulls swooped, dived and screamed when they weren't riding the breeze on motionless wings.

'What happens to me now?' he asked.

'If Taske knows where you live...'

'He doesn't. She won't have told him.' But he didn't sound one-hundred-per-cent sure.

'I won't tell him,' I promised.

'It doesn't matter. Not now. You have the pictures. *And* the negatives.'

'And, friend, you'd better hope that I convince him of *that*.'

170

'Let him know, eh?' There was anxiety in the words.

'Today,' I promised. 'That's the object of the exercise. That's why I came.'

For the last hundred yards or so we ploughed our way forward in silence. We reached the car and I unlocked the door. I shoved the key into the ignition switch, then slipped the Walther from my pocket.

He jumped hard enough to take the soles of his shoes from the shingle.

He spluttered, 'Hey! You said—I mean— You said you *weren't*—'

I pushed him in the chest and he sat down.

My contempt was complete enough not to allow a gramme of pity.

I said, 'You're here because I don't trust you. Not an inch, By my calculations, the nearest telephone is back at your place. I need the time it takes you to get back there. Oh, and one more thing.' I tilted the Walther. 'Try anything funny and if Taske doesn't get you, I *will*.'

He gave a tiny squeal as I squeezed the trigger and sent a round into the shingle about two inches from his balls.

I climbed into the car and drove off. I watched him in the rear-view mirror. He just sat there. He didn't move until I'd rounded a bend and lost sight of him.

The last I saw of him. I think he was crying.

171

*   *   *

I said, 'I've got him. I've got him by the short and curlies.'

And if my voice was a little breathless, it was because I was so sure. So convinced of my hold over Taske.

Bull didn't sound as certain.

He said, 'Take it gently, Harry. You're in Dragon Country. Never forget that.'

I had a pile of 10p pieces with me. I'd already fed three into the slot. I didn't want to be cut off part-way through what I was saying because of a lack of small change.

Bull asked, 'Where are you calling from?'

'A call box. A couple of miles east of Ilkley.'

'A couple of—'

'It's not important. Just that I've got him. By the throat. By the short hairs. Bull, I have *got* him.'

'At a guess, you mean Taske?' Bull made it into a question.

'I have photographs, taken by the clown who billy-goated his wife. Photographs and negatives. Bluer than you'd ever believe. And Taske's wife is there in every one. Thoroughly enjoying herself.'

I told him about my hunch and how it had come off; about Kelly and his gutlessness.

I said, 'He spewed it all out—thought I was there to kill him. He wasn't even sure *I* wasn't from Taske. He's been expecting bad men to

172

call ever since darling Moira phoned him and fixed a meeting. She never made it, of course.'

'Just for a handful of dirty pictures?' Bull didn't sound convinced. He didn't sound too happy.

'You've never seen the like,' I assured him. 'Remember, Kelly was a whiz with a camera. He took his time. Except for what they are, they're all superb shots.'

'For what?' asked Bull. 'What did Kelly want them for, anyway?'

'Memories.' I chuckled, and if it sounded a little like a dirty chuckle, who can fault me. I said, 'Reliving some magnificent moments, I suppose.'

'And you?'

'Me?'

'What are *you* going to do with them?'

'Threaten to sell them to some hard-porn magazine if Taske doesn't come to heel.'

Bull said, 'Oh, God!' and the words weren't far from a groan.

'You haven't seen them, Bull,' I argued. 'You haven't seen anything like them.'

'Harry,' he said heavily, 'I've spent most of my life in the Army. Two spells in the Middle East. I've seen more dirty postcards than you've had hot dinners—and it won't wash. He might not like them being circulated, but it won't stop him. It won't even slow him down.'

'Bull,' I said, 'I don't want them to stop him. Not Kelly's pictures. All I want is for them to

173

get him within shooting distance. *I'll* stop him. Personally.'

It upset him. For an ex-khaki job, he was remarkably averse to bloodshed. He tried hard to talk me out of things; pleaded with me to contact Lyle and let the police take over. I argued with him and eventually said, 'I'll keep in touch. Whatever happens, whatever's going to happen—the lot. The lot. I'll keep you posted. And, friend, don't worry. As far as *I'm* concerned, it's a bit like squashing a bed bug. That's how I feel.'

*   *   *

From Ilkley, it was the A659, through Harewood, Collingham, to the A1 at Boston Spa. West Riding country all the way, and never too far from the muck and grime of the industrial north. And yet, as I'd crossed the high Pennines, around the Skipton area, the landscape had had a Winter Wonderland magic. I'd passed Pendle, home of ancient witches, and their hill had boasted a cloak of frosted snow. The crossroads at Gisburn had been heavy with brown slush, churned up by the heavy goods traffic; Gisburn, home of the wicked and legendary Guy, Robin Hood's sworn enemy. Then up through the tiny villages and hamlets, seemingly clinging with finger-nail precariousness to the steep, snow-heavy slopes. Then, eventually, through

West and East Marton and onto Skipton. From Skipton, past Bolton Abbey, through Addington to Ilkley, with the famous Moor on my right.

And now, having collected my car, I was heading south, along the dual carriageway of the A1.

The A1. The Great North Road. I always counted it as a more homely route than the more modern and swifter M1. Time was, when it groped and snaked its way through townships and villages and, if you didn't know the way, was the very devil to follow. Indeed, time was when it was the haunt of highwaymen and footpads; when it was axle-deep in ruts and mud; when it was hemmed in, on both sides, by great forests. It was The Great North Road when most folk in England (and Scotland) never left the confines of their village of birth throughout their whole life. And now it was a smooth, dual carriageway (a motorway in all but name) and I was hammering south, towards Brotherton and the steaming power station towers of Ferrybridge; under the trans-Pennine motorway and south, towards Doncaster.

The weather gods were undecided. To snow, or not to snow. The sky was gunmetal heavy with the stuff. It stretched, white and featureless, left and right. It was *going* to snow. The only question was 'when'. And, of course, 'for how long'. I decided that the United

175

Kingdom had a cow of a climate.

Just north of Doncaster I swung onto the A1(M) and knew that this was just about the most God-awful twenty miles or so of motorway in the whole network. It crossed the Don valley and, what with industrial gunge mixing with moisture-laden air, there was a fifty-fifty chance of fog. Real, old-fashioned pea-soup stuff. And if it wasn't foggy (which it wasn't) it could drop down, like a pearl-coloured blindfold, in seconds. But (again) it didn't, and I hit the A1 again, north of Blyth, and stopped for a hot meal at the motorway pull-in favoured by so many of the heavy goods boys.

Then it was south for another forty miles or so. Out of Yorkshire. Into Nottinghamshire—a prissy, bloodless county compared with the sod-'em-all harshness of the broad acre county.

Then, at Newark on Trent, east and into Lincolnshire.

Lincolnshire. Bomber County. The spiritual home of Five Group, Bomber Command, during World War Two. Launching ground for some of the greatest—maybe the most infamous—air raids of the war. In those days, one bloody great aerodrome. Dozens of runways. At night, the whole county twinkling and blinking with lights—pundits and beacons—flashing the various code letters of the day, to show the weary flyers their approximate whereabouts.

The Yellow Bellies. The Poachers. And yet, they welcomed the flyers. And those who serviced the planes. The Lancasters. The aeroplane that threatened to nudge the Imp from his logo position representing the county.

And now it was snowing. Deliberately and with a very businesslike persistence. As if somebody was shaking out the contents of a celestial feather pillow.

Lincolnshire. A particularly white and muffled Lincolnshire.

Let me tell you about Lincolnshire.

It is big. It is flat. And, from this county, Five Bomber Group blasted blue crap out of Hitler's Germany. Today, the few oldsters left who flew on those sorties and lived still look upon the county as 'theirs'. They haunt the forgotten homes of the old squadrons. They mooch around the few Lancaster bombers not yet sold for scrap and build beautiful dreams from the tattered memories of once-upon-a-time nightmares.

It is a county of impossible horizons. A place of huge, flat fields and arrow-straight roads.

I was travelling along one of those endless, featureless roads. The A17. Not far from RAF Cranwell, the Air Force's Sandhurst. But there'd be no flying today. No cross-county. Not even 'circuits and bumps'.

I was making for Woodhall Spa and, like most Lincolnshire towns, it was shy. It refused to be 'found' easily. But, through Billinghay, left along the B1192, and I was there.

The Golf Hotel, Woodhall Spa—the place I'd been making for.

*   *   *

The not inconsiderable car park was already two inches deep in snow and getting thicker, but the hotel, standing back from the road behind its own lawns and beds, looked very inviting. I dashed, booked in, then arranged for my bags to be collected and brought to the bedroom I was going to occupy. Meanwhile, I went for a drink. I needed it. I was tired, I was stiff and I was weary of staring at everlasting whiteness.

I downed a double whisky and water, booked dinner, then allowed one of the staff to show me to my bedroom. Room Number 2—on the ground floor: past the bar, through the lounge and a few yards along the corridor. It had twin beds, but, presumably because at that time of year business was outrageously slack, I was offered it as a single room. I had no cause for complaint. My bags had arrived, and I stripped and then soaked in hot, soapy water in the en suite bathroom.

I lay on the bed for about half an hour before I put clothes back on. It was nice. Snoozing. Allowing the bedroom warmth of the central heating to soak itself into my naked body. For

178

the first time in at least forty-eight hours, the tenseness left me and I was able to look ahead with something like confidence, as opposed to wishful thinking.

Bull was the linchpin in my future plans. I knew him. I hoped I knew him well enough. If not, I was down the tubes with a rush.

*   *   *

I ate, slowly and with relish. From the chef's own soup to the coffee and biscuits, I could find no fault. The lamb was done perfectly, the vegetables were fresh and prepared by somebody who knew how and the service was complete and faultless, without being fawning.

Then I returned to my bedroom.

Kelly had given me a telephone number. A nightclub—so he said—and the accepted 'headquarters' of the Taske crowd.

I was a few hundred miles away from them, a few hundred miles from my own home, the bedroom telephone linked directly into the external lines without going through a switchboard—I felt reasonably safe.

The guy at the other end of the wire drew zero marks for telephone technique.

He grunted, 'Yeah?'

'I have a message for Eddie Taske,' I said.

'Eh?'

'Eddie Taske. I have a message for him.'

'Who ain't?'

179

'I don't know who "ain't" ... just that I *have*.'

'So, okay. Gimme the message.'

'Hey, bozo,' I snarled, 'get the Taske man on this blower.'

'Who the hell says?'

'If not, you better start running now,' I warned. 'And Eddie will still catch up with you and ram red-hot pokers up your arse.'

'You talk big.'

'Compared with you, I *am* big,' I bluffed. 'Waste much more of my time and I'll show you *how* big.'

There was a pause, then he said, 'He ain't here. Not at the moment.'

'I just hope you're not pulling funnies.'

'He ain't here. Gimme your number. I'll get him to—'

'No, dumb-bell. I ring *him*. He doesn't ring *me*.'

'Look, I keep telling you. He's not—'

'It's big. It's about his wife,' I interrupted. 'I'll ring every fifteen minutes but, after this evening, it's way gone too late.'

I dropped the receiver and lay back on the bed. In effect, I'd unlatched the door of the cage, and inside the big cats were both hungry and waiting. I must now open the door and face them, or re-lock the door and walk away. Maybe run away and hide. But if I did that, Taske would have won, Liz would almost certainly be in danger and I, personally, was very unlikely to live to a ripe old age.

I checked my watch, left the bedroom and strolled to the bar for another whisky. The customers—locals—were wandering in. They knocked the snow from their shoes at the porch, brushed the scattering of snow from the shoulders of their coats, and looked red-nosed and healthy as they made their way to the bar counter. Christmas wasn't long past. Maybe all of the Dickensian good cheer hadn't quite worn off. I kept glancing at my watch. It *hadn't* stopped and, fifteen minutes, to the second, I was back in my room, sitting on the bed-edge, dialling the London nighterie number.

'This is Edward Taske speaking.'

It was something of a shock. Gangsters equate with side-of-the-mouth mutterings. Slang and bargee talk. Not this one—if indeed it *was* Eddie Taske. There was more than Primary School in his enunciation. More than Grammar School. Somewhere, a Public School had had a hand in training him to voice his thoughts clearly.

I said, 'Eddie Taske?'

'Speaking.'

'Maybe. Maybe not.' I bought time in which to think.

'You must,' he said, 'either take my word for it, or ring off. You left a message, fifteen minutes ago. An urgent message—so you said.'

'Yeah. That's right.'

'You might start by telling me your name.'

'Thompson. Harry Thompson.'

'Ah, yes. Mr Thompson. We haven't yet met, have we?'

'I've met your wife,' I growled. Then added, 'Your *late* wife.'

'Just so.'

'I even have photographs of her,' I said.

'Photographs?'

'Dirty pictures. Lots and lots of dirty pictures. All very specific. All taken by a man who knows how to handle a camera.'

'Mr Kelly?' he murmured.

'*I* have them now. All of them. And the negatives.'

There was a fairly lengthy pause, then he said, 'Let me put it this way, Mr Thompson. What, exactly, can I do for you?'

'Call off the dogs,' I said bluntly.

'Dogs?'

'I'd like to live.'

'All of us, Mr Thompson. All of us.'

'You know what I mean.'

'Not really,' he insisted. Then, 'Are you, by any chance, recording this conversation?'

'Would I tell you?'

'No.' The pause suggested he might be smiling. Then, 'I think that would not have been your reply if you *were* recording.'

'I'm not recording,' I said flatly.

'Therefore?'

'This is strictly between you and me. I'd like to live. I'd like my wife to live. So—call off the dogs.'

'Assuming I know what you're talking about—'

'You know.'

'What do I get from *you*?'

'The photographs.'

'The negatives?'

'Maybe. Maybe not.'

'A point comes to mind,' he said. 'How do I know you *have* them?'

'I'll post one to you tomorrow. One of the less eye-opening. I'll ring you, forty-eight hours from now.'

'And?'

'I'll let you know, then. Any jiggery pokery, and the lot—photographs, negatives, the lot—end up on the desk of some hard-porn magazine. They'll publish, have no fear. They're too good—too *dirty*—for them not to publish.'

'Mr Thompson,' he said, quietly, 'with a modicum of luck, you could live to be a ripe old age. And, of course, your good wife.'

*   *   *

The next day, immediately after breakfast, I drove to King's Lynn. Very cunning. Very crafty. Not even the correct county—that was the big idea.

For some inexplicable reason, I was feeling magnanimous. I included a picture and its

183

negative in the slim parcel. I posted it Next Day Delivery and gave a false name and address to the counter clerk.

Then I worried.

Bull? Lyle? Were they both doing what I counted upon them doing? Was Liz still okay? What about the bodyguard Lyle had promised? I knew about policemen with guns. They have this shooter, but they know that if they use it—regardless of the circumstances—there's a long, drawn-out enquiry. Some poor bastard has to die (well, *almost*) before the armed PC Plod dare squeeze the trigger.

Therefore, I worried.

I worried about Taske. By his voice—by his conversation—Taske had an education. Not just criminal cunning, an *education*. That upset me. It had caught me wrong-footed. Get an animal capable of doing what he'd done to his wife—what he'd done to the poor slob he'd thought was bedding his wife—and you do not expect quiet conversational exchange. You expect strong language. You expect threats and bluff. You expect him to *talk* like a tearaway. And Taske didn't.

And that, too, worried me.

I picked at a perfectly good lunch at the Duke's Head, then crossed the river, found the A17 and started my journey back to Lincolnshire.

It was a long and lonely journey. Way on my right was the Wash and everything else was fields and marshland. In all England—including the Dales and the Peak District—there is nowhere as desolate as East Anglia in mid-winter. The sheer flatness allows the wind to drive and drift the snow without hindrance and the result is a near white-out. Even the traffic was ridiculously light.

I crossed the River Welland and broke the monotony with a coffee at Fosdyke, then it was on, across South Kyme Fen, left at Tattershall and, at last, to my temporary base at Woodhall Spa.

I tried to soak the tiredness out of my limbs, and almost succeeded. Then, I realised how hungry I was and enjoyed a fine dinner and good wine.

Then I mooched to the bar and deliberately tried to get plastered.

It was impossible. I grew maudlin. Then I grew morose and surly. Fortunately, and before any of the other drinkers could pick a quarrel, I weaved my way to Bedroom Number 2, and a deep and surprisingly restful sleep.

*   *   *

I figure you can get used to just about anything. Even the prospect of the chop, in the very near future. Maybe I felt safe and far enough away from Taske and his soldiers. Maybe there is a finite amount of worry and fear which a man is capable of feeling. Maybe anything. Just that, in the cold light of that beautiful and exhilarating morning, the Walther looked a little stupid. A little theatrical, in fact.

The calm before the storm, perhaps? The eye of the hurricane?

I enjoyed a slow and tasteful breakfast. I was in no hurry. I had all day to waste. It had stopped snowing and (or so it seemed) a thaw was setting in.

I took the car out, and drove for the simple sake of driving; as a means of passing time. I drove to Skegness, found it to be one more holiday resort, out of season—cold and inhospitable—then took the road south, to Boston. I lunched at the New England Hotel, and realised that I was developing a taste for good food. I stayed in the panelled bar-lounge as long as was decently possible, then drove north, stopped for a drink at the main pub in Mareham le Fen and ended back at Woodhall Spa in time for a refreshing shower, prior to strolling into the restaurant for dinner. Then it was back to Bedroom Number 2—back to slightly terrifying reality—and my promised call to Edward Taske.

*   *   *

'Ah, Mr Thompson. How nice of you to be so punctual.'

The voice was as smooth and polite as ever. We were two life-long buddies exchanging

186

pleasantries; we were *not* two grown men, each plotting to kill the other.

He'd answered before the third ring had had time to finish. I'd identified myself and now, as far as I was concerned, it was down to business.

I said, 'I take it you received the parcel?'

'Oh, yes. Thank you. Very interesting.'

'Very smutty.'

'That, too, I suppose.'

'You want the rest?'

'I thought we'd already agreed. Of course. If possible.'

'You meet me,' I said.

'Where? When?'

'Alone,' I warned. 'Just you and me.'

'If you insist.'

'I insist.'

'Again: where and when?'

'You know Blackpool?' I asked.

'Vaguely. It's not one of my favourite watering holes.'

'That's where,' I said. 'At the very south end of the prom. A car park—the Star Gate car park.'

'I'll be there. When?'

'Starting tomorrow night. Every night, at twenty minutes past midnight. You walk there. Alone. You wait ten minutes. Then you leave. One night, I'll join you.'

'That's a little involved,' he complained.

'Not really.'

'How long is it likely to go on for?'

187

'Till I'm ready. Till I'm sure.'

'Sure?' He sounded almost offended.

'I don't trust you, Taske,' I said bluntly.

'Eventually,' he replied softly. 'Eventually, you *must*.'

'I'll know when. As you say—eventually.'

'Meanwhile?' he asked.

'Meanwhile, you stroll onto the car park each night at twenty past twelve. You stand there. Alone. Looking out to sea. And you hope I don't get suspicious and send the photographs to some porn publication. And,' I added, 'you keep well clear of both my wife and myself.'

He said, 'There has to be some other way. Some *easier* way.'

'No other way,' I assured him.

'A little bit of trust, perhaps?'

'Trust? I'm told you wouldn't know how to spell the word.'

'I endure vituperation from all angles.'

I had the impression he was quietly taking the mickey out of me.

I said, 'No more talk, Taske. You know what you have to do to get the skin shots of your wife. Be there when I arrive—or else.'

Then I replaced the receiver.

Next I telephoned Bull. I told him what was going to happen. Told him I was visiting the Star Gate car park in three night's time.

'—by that time, he'll have got used to being there, but won't have had time to get bored.'

188

'If he goes there at all.'

'He'll be there.'

'Look...'

'No, *you* look.' I tried to sound irritated. Just enough to push him the way I wanted him to go. I said, 'It's my wife, right? It's my skin, right? So I do it *my* way. Taske's not so tough. Put him on a hot enough grill, he'll fry like the rest of us.' There was a distinct sigh, and I continued, 'You're a nice guy, Bull. You mean well. But I want the bastard *there*. Near enough to get at him.'

*   *   *

I put in an early call and asked for my bill to be ready. By the time the few other guests were enjoying breakfast, I was on my way. Driving towards Newark, then up the A1 and back across the Pennines and onto Home Ground. I stopped for a meal at Clitheroe, then left the main roads and booked in at an isolated inn I knew on the fringe of Bowland Forest. I was within thirty-minutes' drive from the car park and, wherever Taske was staying, I wasn't remotely likely to bump into him. Not even at Blackpool, come to that. Not because of the crowds—Blackpool, at that time of the year, is a cold, inhospitable place. Lonely. Almost deserted. The hoteliers are away, enjoying *their* holidays, and the few people who actually *live* there keep indoors and away from the weather.

189

Nevertheless...

I was contemplating a killing. I wanted as few people as possible to see me at or near the proposed scene.

*   *   *

The next night, I parked the car near the Star Gate park. Off the main promenade road, but with a clear view of the entrance to the car park.

I was there by half-past eleven. I was out of sight; parked on the apron of a row of shops, away from the high-strung lights of the prom and in the gloom of shadows cast by the nearby building.

I wanted to smoke, but didn't. Instead, I eased myself low in the seat, and hoped the car looked appropriately empty to any casual passer-by.

The traffic was light. By midnight, only three people had walked past. At a few minutes after midnight, a police patrol car came up, from the direction of Blackpool, then turned left towards the motorway network.

At twelve-fifteen a taxi pulled in by the kerb. It had come from the direction of Lytham St Annes. A solitary man got out of the cab, paid the driver, then stood on the footpath, as if waiting for other transport, until the taxi had swung in a U-turn and was heading back south. Then the man strolled towards the

190

entrance and entered the car park.

It had to be Taske. Who else?

At half-past twelve, and with the same, slow deliberation he walked back, out of the car park and towards a kiosk at the junction.

I waited until a second taxi arrived from the direction of Blackpool and took him back, towards wherever he had come. Then I enjoyed a deferred cigarette and contemplated Edward Taske, and the first sighting I'd had of him, albeit that sighting from a distance.

Slim, moderately tall and immaculately dressed. This lad was no tearaway. The Crombie overcoat, the gloves, the obviously expensive trilby. That much could be seen, even from a distance. And yet (I reminded myself) this apparently highly civilised man dealt in death, the protection racket and general gang nastiness. There was a certain Yankee, 'The Syndicate' air about him. A certainty. A smooth and quite unhurried assurance that *he*—and nobody else—was in charge.

That, I think, was when I realised that the killing had to be quick. No waiting. No unnecessary conversation. As soon as possible and as quickly as possible.

I finished the cigarette and drove back towards Bowland Forest.

*   *   *

I did not sleep that night. I tried booze. I tried counting sheep. I tried the old remedy of relaxing one muscle at a time. It was no good. In the small hours I suffered stomach cramps, and knew the reason for them. Tomorrow night, I was going to kill.

I was scared. I'd seen the man I was going to kill and that, of itself, made things a hundred times worse. Why? That was a question I was not able to answer. Merely that, had it only been me—had I had a real assurance that Liz wasn't in danger—the whole thing would have been called off.

I stared from the bedroom window of the inn, watched a cloud-racked moon send shadows dancing through the middle-distance trees and wished to hell there was some other way out. I heard the scream of owls and the bark of foxes. I smoked cigarettes without really tasting them—certainly without enjoying them. I saw the sky gradually turn pewter-coloured as a new day arrived.

Then I bathed, dressed and, without offering any sort of excuse, went for a walk in the bitter weather, in the pious hope that it might ease my guts and clear my mind.

It didn't. It merely made me want to puke, until I deliberately took deep, lung-freezing breaths and steadied my nerve and quietened my imagination. I made believe I was not about to commit the ultimate crime in the calendar. I deliberately blocked out the next forty-eight hours of my life. I concentrated my thoughts upon memories of life with Liz; on the pleasant times I'd had with Bull; on the belief that Lyle was a man upon whom to rely.

Then I returned to the inn, enjoyed hot, sweet tea and toyed with scrambled egg on toast.

By mid-morning I was at the Star Gate car park. It seemed much larger than I remembered; possibly the biggest open-air cark park in Blackpool. Alongside the entrance was a single-storey AA office. The parking area was hemmed in by a Go-Kart track, on the seaward side, the tram terminus to the north, a pitch-and-putt golf set-up to the west and a yacht club to the south. There were also toilets, and the promenade ended in a slope, leading from the front itself, down to the surface of the car park. A pock-marked surface; some of it tarmac, some of it muddied dirt, some of it crushed ash.

Three cars were parked in the area. All empty, and nothing to show whether their owners were nearby, or whether they'd all three been abandoned. A solitary, single-decker tram car stood waiting at the terminus; the cream and green livery of Blackpool Corporation looking cold and uninviting in the bitter weather.

And that was all. That and a stray mongrel dog which trotted down the slope leading from the prom. The splash and gurgle of the tide hitting the face of the sea wall could be heard from here. A handful of gulls screamed and wheeled in the light but bitter breeze. It was like the end of the world—the back side of the moon—desolate and cold.

I stayed there perhaps ten minutes, trying to visualise where Taske might stand when I arrived to meet him—to kill him ... but it was an empty and painful exercise.

I drove out of the car park and back onto the promenade road. What to do with my last few hours of freedom. That's what it boiled down to. Come shortly after twelve, tomorrow night, I was going to freeze Taske, then—immediately afterwards—I was going to give myself up. No excuses. No 'Not Guilty' plea. I had the rest of today, tonight and tomorrow. After that, I was going to be surrounded by granite walls.

I would have liked to have spent the time with Liz, but that was out of the question. To go near her might conceivably weaken my already slightly shaky resolve even more. Liz wouldn't see things from my angle—*couldn't* see things from my angle. Therefore, and for her own safety, she had to be kept well away from things.

Bull?

A day with Bull would have been nice, but that, too, would have been risky. Even telephoning him again would have been risky. I thought I knew him; thought I knew what he was doing and what he would do. I hoped to hell I was right, but I daren't over-state things. Push things too far. Try to be *too* tricky.

That was why I spent almost three hours in an almost deserted pleasure park. Blackpool Pleasure Beach. Out of season. *Well* out of season. It was only open at the weekends. Saturdays and Sundays the switchbacks opened a dreamy eye and blinked. The umpteen stalls and booths yawned, stretched, then, come Sunday evening, went back to sleep. Without the people—the punters—the pleasure-seekers—it was a mildly eerie place. A clutter of recently emptied coffins. Tracks that went nowhere, then returned to the spot where they started. A place of odd echoes, like a ballroom with ghostly dancers but no band.

I suspect it fitted my mood, which was why I mooched around the various walkways, collar turned up, hands in pockets and head lowered. The company I wanted, I could not have, therefore I found an odd empathy with this unnaturally desolate place.

But, eventually, I tired, returned to the car and drove into Blackpool for food.

Cod and chips, in a restaurant facing out across the promenade. The pavement, almost deserted, with an occasional group of oldsters—pensioners—having an out-of-season, cheap-rate break at 't'seaside.' The men were bent and slow-moving. The women were white-haired, with new perms and gaudy holiday-style clothes. I watched them with something not too far removed from envy. It was something I had decided to remove from my own life. A decent ending. Something approaching dignity.

On both sides of the carriageway council workers were removing the tag end of last year's Illuminations. Yellow vehicles, and men wearing yellow-coloured weather-jackets. They worked with the steady, unhurried deliberation of all council workers. They worked within areas of traffic-coned safety, as a light weight of traffic passed north and south along the prom.

Drifts of sand had gathered on the walkway of the prom. And the walkway ended with paint-thick, rust-pocked railing; the background for a thousand and one holiday snaps.

It was Blackpool. In or out of season. Still glitzy. Still tasteless and tawdry. But, above all, still *Blackpool.*

With some reluctance, I finished the meal, walked slowly back to the car, then drove inland. Without conscious thought I hit the lesser roads. I drove through villages and hamlets with strange names. Cuddy Hill. Goosnargh. Inglewhite and Chipping. I ended up in Clitheroe, and didn't know how I got there.

In effect, I was going round in circles; killing time, while waiting for the time to kill. The play on words amused me more that it should. I chuckled to myself. Maybe it was more of a giggle than a chuckle. Maybe the pressure was getting at me and making me light-headed.

I smoked the last cigarette in the packet while parked in the rear park of a Clitheroe pub. Then I turned the ignition and slowly— wearily—made my way back to the inn.

*　　*　　*

That evening. That night. The next morning and afternoon. The truth is, I don't know. I can remember nothing with any degree of certainty. I think the weather eased off a little. The cold wasn't quite as hard. I'm almost sure about the weather. Which means I must have been out in the weather ... but I can't remember.

There is a blank. Almost a painful blank which, however hard I try, I cannot fill. There is nothing—*nothing*!—until I remember, with startling clarity, being in the car, on the apron of *The Lemon Tree* pub-cum-casino-cum-roadhouse; an empty pub-cum-casino-cum-roadhouse, with boarded up windows and padlocks on the doors. One of the great white elephants of the Fylde coast.

It was cold but clear. Not quite freezing. Past midnight. The Walther was in my mac pocket. Loaded, and ready for the first squeeze on the trigger. The photographs were in an inside pocket, although why I had brought them was something of a mystery. A possible ploy, perhaps. To get Taske in a better position.

I watched the entrance to the car park. This time, it didn't matter whether or not Taske saw the car. Whether or not he guessed that it was my car. Nothing too much mattered.

This was *it*.

As happened two nights before, he arrived in a taxi. Again, from the direction of St Annes. He alighted, paid the driver, then stood on the footpath until the taxi had U-turned and was on its way back. Then he walked towards the entrance to Star Gate car park.

The Crombie overcoat. The gloves. The trilby. The air of quiet, unhurried certainty.

I left my own car, crossed the promenade road and followed him into the park. I found myself trembling slightly. Hoping to God I hadn't misjudged Bull and his reactions.

The park was a place of half-light and black shadows. A certain amount of backwash from the promenade lights made it a gloomy place. Three cars were parked at the far end of the park. They were all very obviously empty. Nobody else was there—only the solitary figure standing, feet slightly apart and firmly planted, looking out towards the sea.

I soft-footed to within a dozen feet of him then, in a low voice, I said, 'Taske?'

He turned. Deliberately and without haste. In the backwash of light I saw that he was smiling.

He said, 'Who else were you expecting?'

'Nobody else. Just you.'

'And?'

'I'd like your assurance. Your promise.' I was a touch breathless. I didn't want to kill him. Not really. Not if there was another way. I said, 'I'll take your promise. I'll take your word.'

'About what?'

'That you'll leave us alone. My wife and me. That you won't harm us. We know nothing. We can't do you any harm.'

'I'm here to collect some photographs,' he said gently.

'Here.' I pulled the packet of photographs from my inside pocket and tossed them onto the ground, about a yard in front of him. 'They're there. They were an excuse, really. To get you here. To get to talk to you. To—'

'No.'

'Eh?'

'To get *you* here, Mr Thompson.'

His gloved right hand moved from his side and was raised in a tiny gesture. It was nothing. It moved no more than a few inches. But I felt a nudge between my shoulder blades and realised something was wrong. Then I felt a second nudge and, before the fraction of a heartbeat which heralded the incandescent pain, the memories came flooding back. So many memories, in no time at all.

... It was about fifteen minutes into a new day, and I'd driven too far without a break. I'd parked in a quiet corner and was toying with the idea of catnapping before treating myself to tea and a bite before tackling the last fifty miles or so.

I had that warm, satisfied feeling of a job well done. Way back, in the outskirts of Bristol, the refrigeration van had unloaded two sides of cured bacon...

*   *   *

The man being murdered didn't know he was being murdered.

At first it was a push between the shoulder blades. Then it felt as if somebody had kicked him in the back; kicked him, only lightly; kicked him, only lightly; kicked him high up and slightly to the left.

He staggered forward and had a surprised awareness that he was unable to correct his balance; that he couldn't bring his own gun to bear. His last thought was that he might stumble and tear a hole in the knee of his trousers on the crushed ash underfoot.

The rest was memories.

He was dead before he hit the ground.

As the dead man hit the ground the mobile floodlights were switched on and the car park became as well illuminated as the stage in the last act of a pantomime.

A voice, distorted by a loud hailer, bawled, 'Down! You're surrounded. This is the police. Down on the ground, both of you.'

Taske raised his hands to shoulder level. Then, very carefully—almost politely—he lowered himself, first to his knees, then onto all fours.

The middle-aged, smartly-dressed, smiling man—the man who had wasted three shots at Rogate-on-Sands pier head—threw his silencered pistol clear, then rolled out of the boot of one of the parked cars. He ended face downwards, spread-eagled on the surface of the park.

The loud hailer yelled, 'Right down, Taske. On your belly, with your arms wide.'

Taske obeyed, then, from the shadows of the miniature golf links—from the artificial rocks which made up the landward side of the promenade walk—from the hide of the tram terminus shelter—they came. Some quickly. Some not so quickly. Some armed. Some not armed. Uniformed and plain clothes policemen.

One of them, holding a revolver in a two-handed grip, tilted it in line with Taske's back, then kicked his hands even farther apart. Then he stepped around him and kicked his legs farther apart.

He warned, 'Don't try anything, friend. We *want* an excuse to squeeze this trigger.'

A uniformed sergeant raced to the fallen

Thompson. With care and speed he rolled him onto his back, unloosened the tie, the collar and the top button of the shirt and, ignoring the spreading scarlet, bent down and placed his ear to the chest.

Lyle joined him, dropped on one knee and said, 'Get an ambulance. Quick!'

'He's dead.'

'How the hell do *you* know? He might still be—'

'He's dead, sir.' The sergeant straightened. The side of his face was blood-smeared. He said, 'Of course we'll send for an ambulance. But it won't bring him back to life. I'm sorry.'

Lyle's nostrils widened. Then he blew out his cheeks in disgust. Through gritted teeth, he snarled at the dead man.

'You bloody fool, Thompson. You bloody, *bloody* fool. Why in hell couldn't you trust us? Just this once.'

The sergeant stood up, unclipped his personal radio and demanded an ambulance as soon as possible. A plain clothes officer, holding a revolver loosely in one hand, joined them. Lyle spoke to him.

He said, 'Satisfied? We used him as bait. Your idea, remember?'

'You didn't argue too much,' said the newcomer coldly.

'Who argues with the Flying Squad? Who's *allowed* to argue?'

'He pushed himself into everybody's way,

202

Lyle. His nose was a bloody sight too long. Damnation, we warned him off enough.'

'Then you used him.'

'Of course we used him,' said the newcomer angrily. 'At a pinch—unless he was a complete numbskull—he *knew* he was being used.'

'Maybe.'

'Bet on it, friend. Put money on it. Nobody's *so* bloody thick.'

A scream cut through the rest of the noise. The gunman had jerked himself forward and tried to reach his pistol. The uniformed officer who had a handgun trained on the back of his neck stepped smartly to one side, then thudded the heel of his boot into the reaching hand.

The uniformed officer snapped, 'Down, Fido. Don't try any OK Corral antics here.'

The uniformed officer was joined by a plain clothes man who dropped on his knees alongside the still moaning gunman and, while leaving a clear line of fire for the uniformed officer, systematically searched the gunman for other weapons.

Men were searching the two other parked cars. They raced up the slope and flashed beams of powerful torches along the deserted prom and over the sea wall onto the empty sands. They cordoned the car park in order to prevent entry by other vehicles.

The man pointing his gun as Taske said, 'Slowly, friend. Very slowly. Take your hands from the ground and clasp them behind your neck. But *very* slowly.'

Taske was starting to move his hands when the shots rang out.

Three shots. To anyone who'd served in either the 1914–18 war or the 1939–45 war they would have been instantly recognisable. They had a sharp, snapping-of-a-rotten branch peculiarity. It was the sound of standard, British Army, .303 ball ammunition being fired from a Short, Magazine, Lee-Enfield rifle.

The first bullet smashed Taske back onto the surface of the car park.

He gasped, 'You bast—'

The second bullet silence him and rolled him half over.

The third bullet made Taske's body give a single twitch as it struck.

The police officer swung round, still holding the revolver in a two-handed grip. The combination of floodlights and headlights blinded him and, for a moment he looked both helpless and confused. Within the circle of lighted car park the other officers looked equally bewildered.

Lyle straightened and raced for the gloom beyond the southern edge of the light's perimeter. He switched on a three-battery torch and shone its beam through the link wire and into the yacht club's grounds.

He shouted, 'You're in there somewhere. Don't be a damned fool. Whoever you are, you're pinned in.'

A plain clothes officer joined him, and said, 'Did they come from—'

'I think so. From where I was, they seemed to.'

'We're something of an easy target, standing here,' said the plain clothes officer uneasily.

'Possibly,' grunted Lyle.

'In that case—'

'If it's who I think it is, he won't shoot coppers.'

'Oh!'

Lyle raised his voice, and called, 'Don't make it into a shoot-out. Just come out quietly. It's the sensible thing to do.'

There was a sound and Lyle tilted the beam of the torch upwards. It illuminated the rifle as it cartwheeled to earth from the flat roof of the yacht club.

Bull Adams shouted, 'That's it, Lyle. The only weapon I have. And the rest of the ammunition is in the magazine.'

'Give yourself up, Adams.'

'Of course. That's what I intended to do. I've done what I came for.'

* * *

The motorcade made its way sedately along the promenade. It was headed by a Lancashire County Patrol car. Then came the superintendent's car, followed by a Flying Squad car in which sat Adams and Lyle. It, in turn, was followed by a second squad car and, finally, a second Flying Squad car. The whole looked more like a fairly hurried funeral procession rather than police vehicles leaving the scene of a shooting.

Lyle was handcuffed to Adams, in the rear of the car. A Flying Squad sergeant sat in the front passenger seat and a Flying squad constable drove.

Lyle said, 'I'm not supposed to ask you questions. You realise that, do you?'

The squad sergeant half turned, and said, 'He's been cautioned.'

'Three times,' grunted Adams. 'A uniformed copper when I was halfway down the ladder. A uniformed sergeant when they clapped the cuffs on me. And Laddo, in front, when they pushed me into this car.'

'You know where you stand,' growled the sergeant.

Lyle said, 'If you *do* care to say anything.'

He made it sound like a question. Maybe an invitation.

Adams said, 'I was sure it was going to be Taske who did the shooting. I was bloody *sure.*'

'So were we.'

'I was ready to drop Taske the second he put a hand into his pocket. That's how sure I was.'

'That's understood.' Lyle paused, then continued, 'Taske didn't even have a gun with him.'

'Not Taske. But the other bastard. Taske didn't *need* a gun.'

'True.'

Quietly, and with absolute conviction, Adams said, 'Thompson set it all up, of course. Not me. But he counted on you lot being there.'

'It's possible.'

'It's certain. He told me everything. Even about tonight, and what time. He knew damn well I'd tell you—and he knew damn well what *you'd* do.'

'We stood by and let him get killed,' said Lyle sourly.

'Not so.' The sergeant sounded quite angry. 'If the man had even half co-operated—if he'd even—'

'Sergeant, he's bloody dead,' snapped Lyle. 'Your conscience may be elastic enough to take that sort of strain. Mine isn't.'

'He could have let us know.'

'He *did* let you know.' Adams's voice was a quiet snarl. 'He let *me* know, knowing that I'd let *you* know. Hell's teeth! Do you want postcards?'

They drove in silence the time it took the motorcade to travel between the Pleasure Beach and Waterloo Road.

Then Adams asked, 'Did I kill him?' He paused, gave a quick half-smile, and added, 'I meant to. I don't have to tell you that.'

Lyle looked worried, and said, 'You'd better

not say much more till you see a solicitor.'

'He's not dead.' Adams pressed the point.

The sergeant answered, 'The paramedic says he might live.'

'You smashed his spine,' added Lyle. 'We're told the surgeons might be able to mend things—a little, at any rate.'

Adams murmured, 'Damn! And I won cups for shooting in the army.'

Again there was silence until they reached the Central Pier, waited at the traffic lights, then turned right, inland, towards the police station.

Adams asked, 'The sod who killed Harry. You've taken good care of him?'

'Manser,' said Lyle quietly. 'Edward Arnold Percival Manser. We know him. Well. He's bought himself a hundred-acre, private fertiliser farm. To deliberately shoot a man in the back, with a dozen or so coppers as witnesses. I've known of wiser capers.'

The motorcade slowed its speed as it turned left and into the precincts of Blackpool Police Station.

Lyle said, 'That's enough for now, Adams. There'll be a session in an interview room. Maybe more than one session. You'll get a fair shake. Just don't show too much eagerness.'

PART THREE

'Not just dirty pictures, of course,' said Lyle. 'Not *just* dirty pictures. I think even Thompson had gumption enough to know that. Dope. That was at the bottom of things. The drug barons were seeking an outlet in the UK. The Taske Force had the network, but things hadn't been finalised.'

The Assistant Chief Constable (Crime) grunted. He made no comment, if only because he didn't want to make himself sound the prat he was. He'd popped across to Rogate-on-Sands to clue himself up with the ins and outs of the glorified pantomime which had taken place at Blackpool the previous night, and Lyle had escorted him on a quiet stroll along Rock Walk in order to fill in the finer details.

Lyle said, 'The Squad boys had things in hand. More or less. Then Thompson arsed things up generally, by picking up the Taske woman. The Squad boys were very upset.'

'The Squad boys,' grunted the ACC (Crime), 'get upset rather easily.'

'Can't blame them,' said Lyle magnanimously. 'They were working with the Yankee drug enforcement crowd. Then in comes Thompson and re-jigs everything.'

'You say he was going to shoot Taske? Thompson? His intention was to shoot Taske?'

'Not much doubt.' They moved slowly along the tarmac path which snaked its way alongside the artificial stream which, in turn, divided Rock Walk into two halves. Lyle continued, 'At a guess, he never realised the size of the tiger he was riding. They'd tried to bomb him in his car, but it went wrong. Instead they smashed his wife up a little. Maybe he was scared. Maybe it was some sort of revenge. Whatever, he'd every intention of gunning down Taske.'

'And Taske knew it?'

'Probably. Probably guessed. For sure he wasn't intimidated by the porn photographs. His wife was a whore before he married her. He runs a fair slice of the London prostitution rackets. A few billy-goat snapshots aren't going to make him come out in a hot flush. He went to the car park because he *wanted* to go to the car park.'

'To shoot Thompson.'

'To have Thompson shot,' corrected Lyle.

In some of the corners of the artificial rocks a residue of fallen snow still fought off the salt in the air. The grass looked squashy, with worm casts here and there. The soil of the empty flower beds was heavy and soaked. Come spring the tulips would stand in guardsman-like rows, the crocuses would dapple the green with purple, white and yellow, the daffs would cluster in banks around the trees. Rock Walk would be worthy of being the background to a thousand-and-one holiday snaps. But, now, all it had to offer was privacy.

The ACC (Crime) still looked puzzled.

He said, 'It doesn't make sense. Have his wife killed. Have Thompson killed. But *why*?'

'They're not like us.' Lyle's tone was laced with patience. 'They mistrust everybody. *Everybody*. Wives, brothers, members of the family. His wife knew something was on the point of being finalised. Something big. How much she knew, we can only surmise. But she found *something* out. She was on her way to Kelly—one of the few people *she* could trust— followed by Q cars from the squad. She stopped off at a motorway service area ... and we know the rest.'

'Good God!'

'A murder—*two* murders, actually; Thompson shot a man here, at Rogate.'

'Hell's teeth ... *no*!'

'At his wife's place,' continued Lyle. 'Not counting an attempted murder by bombing. Adams' attempted murder of Taske. And, of course, Manser's killing of Thompson.'

'Who the hell is Manser?'

'The gunman. The bastard hiding in the boot of the car.'

'Oh!'

The path ended. They did a sauntering about turn and started back the way they had come.

'Quite a blood-bath,' observed the ACC (Crime).

'Nothing needs detecting,' said Lyle.

213

'Quite.'

'In some ways—in *many* ways—Thompson brought it on himself.'

'You think so?'

'Too meddlesome. A personal opinion, of course, and I'm sorry about the outcome ... but that's what it boils down to.'

'I suppose.'

There followed about twenty yards of slow-paced silence then, for no reason at all, and without any meaning whatever, the ACC (Crime) grunted, 'Quite. Eh?'

And that was it. The end. Finis. Kaput.

All, that is, (and as Lyle reminded Cullpepper) except the business of the stolen sides of bacon...

*   *   *

'Eh?' Cullpepper stopped, mid-stride, half-way towards the door.

'The business of the sides of bacon,' repeated Lyle.

They were in Lyle's office. The small hours of past midnight were ticking past and, at Cullpepper's suggestion, they'd just gone over the ins and outs of the shoot-up at Star Gate car park.

'I don't get you.' Cullpepper turned and once more faced Lyle.

'Take a seat,' suggested Lyle. 'It's a subject well worth a discussion.'

Cullpepper scowled a little then, with a show of reluctance, returned to the chair he'd just vacated.

Lyle leaned back in his desk chair, clasped his hands behind his neck and, without hurry, but without hesitation, began to speak.

'North of England Pork Products. They called in here a couple of weeks back—maybe more—and complained about the theft of bacon.'

'I still don't see—'

'You remember, of course. You happened to be at the public counter at the time. They complained to you. The manager—a Mr Roebottom—knows you by sight. He complained. He's quite certain. He spoke to *you.*'

Cullpepper's face was expressionless. He said nothing. He merely waited.

'You were busy at the time,' continued Lyle. 'That was the day—if I've got things right—the day following the ram-raid on the Main Street jewellery shop. Remember?'

'I was busy,' growled Cullpepper. 'A four thousand quid smash and grab. A few slices of bacon lifted. There has to be a sense of priorities, otherwise we wouldn't know up from down—hell from arsehole.'

'I don't think you even logged it,' said Lyle. 'You certainly didn't take a Complainant's Statement from the manager.'

'Like I say—'

215

'Like *I* say. You didn't even log it. As far as this nick is concerned it didn't happen. The bacon *wasn't* lifted.'

'A few slices of—'

'A few *sides*,' interrupted Lyle.

'Ah!'

'You didn't know that, of course?'

'No. I didn't *know* that.'

'You didn't ask.'

'Hell, what with the raiders—and the other bits and pieces of that day—it didn't seem too urgent. Nothing to get excited about.'

'You pick your crime, do you?' The question was laced with a hint of sarcasm. 'You decide what you're going to report—what you're going to log—and what you're going to ignore.'

'Is this—' Cullpepper swallowed. 'Is this a reprimand?'

'Not yet.' Lyle's lips curled into a cold, quick smile. 'I'll let you know what it is. Believe me, you'll be left in no doubt.'

'I—er—I think I should be warned,' growled Cullpepper.

'Warned?'

'Y'know ... *warned.*'

'D'you mean "cautioned"? "You're not obliged to say anything"? All that garbage?'

'The rules say so.'

'You know "the rules", of course?'

'Aye.' Cullpepper nodded.

'So it's not needed, is it? You know it, you

216

understand it, you know how it goes, without anybody wasting time saying it.'

'I reckon.'

'Let's take it as read. Right?' Then, like a playful cat teasing a helpless mouse, 'Not that it's necessary. Not yet. You'll know when you should be cautioned, Cullpepper. You'll know. You won't have to be told.'

Cullpepper waited. He looked a little worried, but tried to hide his concern.

Lyle said, 'You had Thompson in. Shortly after he'd returned from sorting out the bacon theft you'd ignored.'

Cullpepper nodded.

'Shortly after Taske's wife was killed.'

Again, Cullpepper nodded.

Lyle asked, 'Why?'

'Eh?'

'Why drag him in? Why insist upon it in the small hours?'

'I was making enquiries. About crime.'

'Which crime?'

'Crime ... generally.'

'Bullshit.'

'Look, you can't—'

'I bloody well *can*,' snapped Lyle. 'Anything. I carry the rank. Don't forget that, Sergeant. What you were after—what you were "enquiring" about—was Thompson's recent movements. Where he'd been. Who he'd seen.'

'Like I say ... crime enquiries.'

'For Taske, eh?'

'Taske?' The name seemed to stop at the back of Cullpepper's throat.

Lyle leaned forward, rested his forearms on the desk top, steepled his fingers and spoke coldly, quietly and with absolute certainty. This wasn't cat-and-mouse tactics. This was the kill.

He said, 'Cullpepper, you won't be the first bent copper. Nor the last. Operation Countryman exposed the extent of the corruption in the Met. It still goes on. We both know the truth of it.

'The other night. We—the police—were at the Star Gate car park an hour before Taske was due to arrive. A good hour. Three cars—I think I've told you. Three cars, parked there. They stay there every night. The local police know them. Vehicles belonging to people who live nearby. But Manser—the man who killed Thompson—came from the boot of one of those cars. Hiding in the boot. He must have been there when we arrived.

'Think about it, Cullpepper.' The tone was as smooth as silk. As sharp as a razor. 'There's a limit to the length of time you can spend in the boot of a car. Cramped up. Suffering from some degree of claustrophobia. The boot open a little, obviously. Enough to give some air. Enough to give a view of the man you're there to kill for. Taske.

'And you'd better watch. Watch closely.

Because Taske hasn't a gun, but Thompson has. Taske's risking things. He might even be putting his life on the line, in the hope that Thompson will die before Thompson can kill. A gamble, wouldn't you say?'

Lyle paused long enough to take a packet of cigarettes from his pocket. He chose and lighted a cigarette. He didn't offer one to Cullpepper.

Cullpepper stayed silent, but his expression left little doubt about the effect of Lyle's words.

Lyle said, 'Taske knew. Everything. The day, the time, the place. The police set-up. Everything. And how did he know?'

Lyle inhaled and exhaled cigarette smoke, then continued, 'He knew, because Thompson kept Adams informed, and Adams kept *us* informed. Maybe that's what Thompson wanted. Maybe. But, sure as hell, he didn't want one of *us* to keep Taske informed. Not that. Anything but that.

'But Taske had feelers, eh? That first day— the day—the night—Thompson picked up his wife. That's when Taske wanted to know things. That's when he sent his feelers out. That's when he offered you ... whatever it was he offered you. That's when you *accepted* it. That's when you were trapped.'

Like a hot wind rustling dry leaves, Cullpepper's voice said, 'You'll never prove it, Lyle. You'll *never* prove it.'

'Give me an hour with Manser,' drawled Lyle. 'Give me an hour with Taske—his back's gone but, with luck, he'll reach a wheelchair one day. Give me an hour with *him*. The rest of my life, Sergeant. I'll nail you. Taske and Manser will drop you. Don't ever doubt that. Adams will *certainly* want you buried.

'Let me remind you. We're not talking dirty pictures any more. We're talking dope. Drugs. We're talking murder and attempted murder. You're lost, Sergeant. You are *lost*.'

They sat in silence for a few moments, then Cullpepper stood up from the chair. Slowly. Wearily.

In a voice which didn't sound like his own, he said, 'I'm finishing. I'm going home.' Then, 'you'll have my resignation on your desk later this morning.'

'It won't save you.' Lyle's tone was flat; expressionless and without mercy. He said, 'This isn't something that's going to be swept under the carpet, Cullpepper. You knew what you were doing. You knew what would happen if you were found out. It's happened, and it's *going* to happen. That's all.'

Cullpepper left the office. Lyle sat there, smoking his cigarette. He squashed the butt out in an ash-tray, but still sat there. Suddenly, he looked an old and tired man.

PART FOUR

'My client...' The defence barrister started speaking before he was fully upright. He unfolded himself from the chair in the well of the court, grasped the lapels of his cloak to hitch it more firmly across his shoulders and, momentarily, glanced at the dock, before turning his full attention onto the witness box and its occupant. He said, 'My client, the accused man, Manser. How well did you know him, Superintendent?'

'Hardly at all.' Lyle's answer was flat and expressionless. It answered the question, and nothing more. This was the cross-examination, and the man conducting the defence was one of the best in the business. Certainly one of the best on the circuit, and Lyle was a good enough copper to know that the case against Manser was still a little tattered at the edges.

The barrister smiled and added, 'Not—how do you put it in police circles, Superintendent? ... not from your manor. Is that it?'

'I understand he's from London.'

'Indeed.' The barrister nodded. 'He is from London. As, also, is one of the previous witnesses, Edward Taske.'

'Yes, sir.'

'I'm told they are great friends. Did you know that?'

'I, too, was told that.'

'Just as you and the deceased—Harry

Thompson—were great friends.'

'I wouldn't put it quite like that.'

'No?'

'We knew each other. Little more than that.'

'Only "knew each other"?'

'That's all.'

'And yet, you were present when he was shot?'

'Yes.'

'Despite the fact that the shooting took place well out of your own police district?'

'Yes.'

'Why?'

'Sir?'

The defence barrister put on a slightly pained—slightly long-suffering—expression and, half-addressing the jury, said, 'Superintendent, I am quite sure the court would be interested to know *why*—when it was well out of your own police district—you saw fit to be present when Thompson was shot?'

'I was following a certain line of enquiry, sir.'

'Be more specific, please.'

'Crime committed at Rogate-on-Sands.'

'Even *more* specifically?'

'A murder and a bombing.'

'To do with my client?' asked the defence barrister, innocently.

'No, sir.'

'To do with the deceased? Thompson?'

'To do with Thompson.'

The pause in the exchange was quite

deliberate. It was created by the defence barrister leaning across and picking up a transparent envelope from the exhibits table.

He straightened, moved his body to show that, technically, he was addressing the next few words to the judge and jury.

He said, 'I take Exhibit Number Seven.' Then, to Lyle, 'Exhibit Number Seven, Superintendent. Photographs. Remarkably indecent photographs which, according to a previous witness, Thompson removed from his pocket and threw to the ground just before he was shot.'

'Yes, sir. I've seen them.'

'Very indecent photographs, wouldn't you agree?'

'Indeed.'

'Tell the court, Superintendent. Do you recognise any of the people in those photographs?'

'The woman is the wife of the witness, Taske.'

The judge leaned forward a little, and murmured, 'Mr Hing.'

'M'lud?' Hing raised questioning— surprised—eyebrows.

'This line of questioning has a purpose, I presume?'

'M'lud, the purpose of these questions will become crystal clear in a very short time.'

'I am obliged, Mr Hing. I look forward to some surprisingly crystal clarity in the very near future.'

Having indulged in this gentle forensic exchange, Hing turned his attention back to Lyle.

He said, 'Dirty pictures, showing the wife of the witness Taske in some quite amazingly compromising situations. And the deceased met Taske, in the middle of the night, at a deserted car park. Strange ... wouldn't you say, Superintendent?'

'Unusual,' agreed Lyle.

'And that you witnessed that meeting. Again ... strange?'

'I was with other officers. We were on duty.'

'What *sort* of duty?'

'Acting on information received,' said Lyle stiffly.

'I see.' The hint of a sneer was ever so gentle. 'And, of course, you are not prepared to disclose to the court the identity of your informant?'

'I'm sorry, sir.'

'But you did know about the photographs?'

'I was told.'

'More "information received"?'

'Yes, sir.'

'You were told they were in the possession of the deceased, Thompson?'

'Yes, sir.'

'Tell me, Superintendent.' The question was silky smooth, and deadly. 'Do you encourage blackmail?'

226

'No, sir.'

'That's what was happening.'

'It would seem so, sir.'

'Thompson was blackmailing Taske.'

'If you say so.'

'Can you offer the court a better explanation?'

'No, sir.'

'Thompson was blackmailing Taske,' repeated the defence council. Then, 'The previous witnesses—police witnesses—all agree that that was why this midnight meeting was arranged. Thompson *was* blackmailing Taske.'

'Yes, sir,' said Lyle unhappily.

'What is more...' Hing again leaned toward the exhibits table and picked up the Walther pistol, in its Cellophane bag. He held it slightly aloft as he continued, 'Thompson saw fit to carry a loaded firearm at that meeting.'

Lyle did not answer.

'This.' Hing held the Walther a little higher. A *loaded* pistol. Tell me, Superintendent ... why?'

'I don't know.'

'Give the court the benefit of an educated assumption, please.'

Lyle paused, moistened his lips, then said, 'He was—he was a member of a responsible gun club.'

'He had a firearms certificate, of course?'

'Yes, sir.'

'Therefore, licenced to possess?'

'Yes, sir.'

'But *not* licenced to carry, loaded, on the Queen's highway?'

'No, sir.'

'Much less—to use an expression—licenced to kill?'

'No, sir. Of course not.'

'And yet—forgive me, Superintendent—I understand you have reason to believe that he *did* kill?'

*   *   *

At the back of Preston Crown Court a group of police officers suffered in sympathy with Lyle. It was an impossible situation, and Hing was merciless in his determination to shift as much distaste as possible from his client, Manser. To make witnesses squirm; to make them obviously uncomfortable. That was his task, and he was a past master at the art. To curve the questions in order to give the answers the appearance of evasion—that, too, was part of the black craft of cross-examination. And Hing was a master craftsman.

Some of the men—those from the Lancashire Constabulary—had suffered at the hands of this superb practitioner.

A police constable muttered, 'Why doesn't he tell the court what a bastard he is?'

A Flying Squad officer snorted, 'Christ

228

Almighty!'

'He can't,' explained a Lancashire sergeant. 'The rules of evidence, son.'

'I don't see why—'

'As white as virgin snow, lad. Even animals like Manser and Taske. Until they're found guilty, they haven't a stain on their beautiful pinnies.'

The Lancs sergeant murmured, 'And if he took a flyer, and slipped in some remark about Manser being a ring-tailed sod, the judge would direct the jury to ignore that remark.'

'Yeah.' A Flying Squad officer chuckled quietly. 'And *wouldn't* they?'

'It could mean a re-trial. Hing would try for one. And re-trials just about guarantee an acquittal.'

The uniformed inspector hissed, 'Quiet, you lot. Lyle's doing his best. He's being hung out to dry—but who wouldn't?'

*   *   *

'Tell the court about the killing you suspect Thompson of committing,' said Hing.

'Mr Hing.' The judge sounded quite cross. 'I am at a loss to see how the deceased's ballistic idiosyncracies have any bearing on the guilt, or innocence, of your client.'

'The difference between that guilt, or that innocence, m'lud,' said Hing smoothly.

'Really! I fail to see—'

229

'At the very least, the difference between the crime of murder and the crime of manslaughter.'

'There is a limit to the liberties I am prepared to allow,' warned the judge.

'Quite so, m'lud,' then, without any real pause, Hing continued, 'Now, Superintendent, will you please tell the court—in your own words—why you suspect the deceased of committing a murder.'

'He told us,' said Lyle, flatly.

'*Told* you?'

'He telephoned the witness Adams and told him. Adams told the police, and the bullet from the victim matches a sample bullet fired from that gun.'

'Thompson's gun?'

'Yes, sir.'

'Now, why on earth should Thompson kill somebody? Do you have any ideas?'

'He disturbed him burglarising his wife's house.'

'"He" being Thompson?'

'Yes, sir.'

'"His wife's house" meaning *Thompson's* wife's house?'

'Yes, sir.'

'Not *his* house? Not *Thompson's* house?'

'No, sir. They lived apart.'

'Was Thompson's wife at home at the time?'

'No, sir.'

'The house was empty?'

'Yes, sir.'

'And yet, he shot a stranger?'

'A burglar, caught in the act.'

'Quite ... but a stranger?'

'Yes, sir.'

'And *not* in his own house?'

'In his wife's house.'

'Not in his *own* house?'

'Not in his own house.'

'In a quite empty house?'

'The house was empty, sir.'

'Amazing!' Hing looked suitably amazed.

Lyle stayed silent.

In an off-handed, throw-away tone, Hing said, 'But, of course—as you know—Thompson was, shall we say, eccentric.'

The judge interrupted, 'I hear what you say, Mr Hing.'

'M'lud?'

'My leniency is not without its limits.'

'M'lud, I wish to make it clear to the court that the deceased was not "normal", as you, or I—as members of the jury—understand that expression.'

'You have witnesses to prove that point?'

'I have the present witness, m'lud.'

'Is the state of the deceased's mind relevant?'

'M'lud, he was carrying a gun. A *loaded* gun. He was committing blackmail. My submission is that his state of mind is very relevant. At the very least relevant enough to reduce the charge to one of manslaughter.'

'I repeat. My leniency has limits.'

'I will bear that in mind, m'lud.' Hing turned to the witness box and continued, 'Thompson was separated from his wife?'

'Yes.'

'Divorced?'

'Yes.'

'Do you know the grounds for the divorce?'

'He had a breakdown.'

'You *know* that?'

'It was fairly common knowledge among his friends.'

'But...' Hing frowned. 'I understand, from your previous answers, that you and he *weren't* friends?'

'I said we were not *great* friends.' The impression was that Lyle was back-pedalling slightly.

'Friends enough to know the reason for his divorce?'

'Yes.'

'And the reason was, because he had a breakdown?'

'Yes.'

'A nervous breakdown?'

'Yes.'

'And yet,' mused Hing, 'He had been issued with a Firearms Certificate. Had he not?'

'He was a member of a gun club. He must have held a Firearms Certificate.'

'Was that wise, do you think? A personal opinion, of course.'

Lyle spoke carefully. He said, 'For myself, I would have hesitated before I'd have recommended the chief constable to grant a Firearms Certificate. I would have, at least, suggested that the issue be temporarily refused. Say for four or five years, then it could have been the subject of another application.'

'In other words, he was not mentally stable enough to be trusted with a firearm?'

'Something like that,' agreed Lyle, hesitantly. He was about to add a rider, but Hing interrupted.

He said, 'That is the end of my cross-examination, m'lud. I thank you for being so tolerant.'

The prosecuting barrister made as if to stand up for a re-examination, changed his mind and remained seated.

*   *   *

Hing was riding wide and at full throttle. His closing speech to the jury had come after four packed days of evidence. At first, it had seemed clear cut. Manser had fired bullets from the Llama pistol. Those bullets had struck Thompson in the side and the back and, as a result, Thompson had fallen to the ground, dead.

Murder?

But, of course. And, moreover, in the presence of a whole crowd of police witnesses.

And yet—and yet...

'... Thompson had already killed. He had shot a complete stranger to death. He had committed that ultimate crime in the unoccupied home of his estranged wife. Members of the jury, please bear that simple fact in mind. We are not here to reach a verdict on the death of an innocent, God-fearing man. Oh, no! A killer, no less...

'... I put it to you that the mental state of the man killed, in this case, is just as important as the mental state of the man accused of the killing. And the man killed was mentally unstable. A senior police officer has given evidence to that effect. A police officer who was present at the scene when the accused committed whatever crime you find him guilty of. If, indeed, you conclude—and without some reasonable doubt—that he, in fact, *committed* a crime...

'We must remember that the witness Taske and the accused man were great friends. They were—still are remarkably close. That must be borne in mind throughout all your deliberations. Two men. Like brothers. In some way closer than many brothers...

'... Blackmail. Not a very savoury crime. Indeed, a quite disgusting crime. And especially so when the victim is a man trying to defend the honour of his wife. You have seen the photographs. And if, like me, you are disgusted by them, try to imagine what your feelings would be supposing somebody threatened to expose in a public newspaper similar photographs of somebody close to *you*. Your wife. Your husband. Your daughter. Consider your emotions should such a situation arise...

'... and remember—never forget, while you are considering the degree of guilt apportioned to the accused man, Manser—that this whole incident was the result of illegalities committed by the deceased. The accused would not be in the dock, you and I would not be here, this whole case would never have been brought, if the dead man, Thompson, had behaved reasonably and legally. *He* was the springboard via which the witness Taske was crippled for life. The reason why the man Adams shot Taske. Indeed, the reason for it *all*...

'... a man capable of killing. A man who had already killed. At midnight, in a deserted car park. And the accused's great friend, Taske, faced by this armed killer. I suggest that the circumstances are such that the only moral crime committed was foolishness. A foolishness which prompted the accused to hide himself—to arm himself—and keep a watchful eye on a friend he counted to be in danger...

'... a mixture of illegalities, stupidities and acceptable errors. I put it to you that we have faults on all sides, but that the basic *wrongs*—

the wrongs from which stem this whole case, the death, the injuries, *everything*—can be placed squarely at the doors of the deceased man, Thompson, and the witness Adams. That when the police are present, in force, at the scene of a shoot-out and do nothing to prevent a killing and a maiming, then at least a part of that fault—the fault which resulted in this sad state of affairs—must be apportioned to them. They stood by while a known murderer committed flagrant blackmail. They watched while the friend of the man being blackmailed went to extreme lengths in an honest belief that he was saving his friend from being murdered. They did nothing while a man with a service rifle pumped bullets into the back of an innocent man. I put it to you that, without even reasonable doubt, the police *and* the deceased, Thompson, carry whatever burden of guilt the evidence put forward in this case has established ...'

*   *   *

Consider a jury room. It is just about the most ridiculously contrived area ever thought up by man. It is unnatural. It is completely artificial—and yet the theory has it that the jury room represents one of the bulwarks of English Criminal Law.

But in a jury room there can never be ambiguity. Within its confines reservations are not allowed. Only guilt or innocence; black or white; up or down.

The pundits prate about 'reasonable doubt', but without defining the limits, or limitations, of that expression. With a known liar, 'reasonable doubt' is attached to every sentence uttered. With an archbishop there is, at least, a degree of certainty that untruths are only accidental.

Yet the evidence of all men is similar when examined in a jury room. It either does, or it doesn't—it is, or it is not—it can never be accidentally slanted because of a mood, or a belief, or a point of view. And, if it is, that mood—that belief, that point of view—must not be openly acknowledged.

Everybody speaks the truth.

Everybody hears and understands.

There are no grey areas; everything is black or white.

Thus the theory behind the jury system; thus the delusion within the jury room.

*　　*　　*

The jurywoman said, 'I'll go along with the rest of you. If he *was* a blackmailer I can't see why we should have much sympathy for him.'

The juryman said, 'I'm sorry. I'm a bit hard of hearing. I didn't quite catch everything. But, from what I *did* hear...'

The sheep farmer called for jury service said,

'Look, let's get it done with. We've wasted four days here already.'

The retired pharmacist called for jury service said, 'I think we should back the police. They have a thankless job these days. I think we should bring in a verdict they would approve of.'

The hairdresser called for jury service said, 'He dresses very neatly. Takes care with his personal appearance, that's what I mean. I can't think a man like that can be a criminal.'

The musician called for jury service said, 'I've lost three gigs already. What they give as expenses won't cover that. Bet money on it.'

The builder, who was foreman of the jury, said, 'Let's have a show of hands, eh? First impressions. Then we can argue the pros and cons between ourselves.'

The sheep farmer said, 'Hey up! I've some lambing to see to. I don't want to waste another day arguing about a lot of nowt.'

The jurywoman said, 'I really don't mind. Whatever everybody else thinks. I don't mind.'

The accountant called for jury service said, 'Really! We should take it seriously, you know. Each express an opinion, and the reason for that opinion.'

The deaf juryman said, 'Eh? What's that you say?'

The PR man called for jury service said, 'Christ, I've been dying for a smoke for the last two hours. Does anybody mind?'

238

The jurywoman said, 'Just don't blow it in my direction, that's all.'

The hairdresser said, 'What's the chance of a cup of tea in this place? Does anybody know?'

The foreman said, 'For heaven's sake, let's do *something*. Let's at least have a show of hands.'

The journalist called for jury service said, 'Those lawyers make a meal of it, don't they? I thought that defence council was never going to pack it in.'

The pharmacist said, 'They all have verbal diarrhoea. That's why it's taken so long.'

The foreman said, 'Look. *Look*! Let's have a show of hands. That's all. But let's start *somewhere*, or else we'll never get home.'

*   *   *

Lord Justice Littlebright was both outraged and annoyed. And he saw no reason for hiding his annoyance. He scowled at the foreman of the jury, glanced scornfully at the defence council, glared open displeasure at the man in the dock, then returned his attention to the jury box.

'And that is your majority verdict?' he demanded.

'It is, my lord.' The foreman bobbed his head, then sat down.

'The law,' growled Littlebright, 'demands that I accept your verdict. I do so. But the law does not preclude me from making certain observations, and if those observations find their way into print in various national newspapers, I will have no objection.'

He took a deep breath, then continued, 'It has been said that the law is an ass. In the main I do not subscribe to that belief. But, today, I have witnessed an example of asinine appraisal beyond anything I have encountered in all my years at the bar and on the bench.

'A "Not Guilty" judgement is almost beyond belief, even when that verdict is not unanimous. In my opinion such a verdict— even though it be a majority verdict—is a verdict in face of all the evidence.

'It is said—and I agree with the saying—that the strength of the English legal system is based on the near-certainty that although many guilty men go free, the system ensures that very few innocent men are punished. That is as it should be. *But* to see a blatantly guilty man escape in this way is, equally, a mockery of the system.

I therefore record your verdict, but I also record my own shock and displeasure at that verdict. And as for *you*...'

The judge turned and glared his annoyance at Manser. 'I am obliged to allow you to step from the dock, and leave this court a free man. I assure you, I am loth so to do, but have no choice. But—and you would do well to ponder on my words—if ever I find myself officiating in a court where you have been accused and found guilty ... beware. I personally, will ensure that the full force of the law will descend upon you, without an atom of mercy.'

*   *   *

Lyle said, 'You win some, you lose some.'

'Not so.' Liz Thompson's voice carried angry indignation. 'Harry was gunned down by that animal Manser. And in front of a posse of police witnesses. Good God, he was *guilty*. Guilty as hell. The judge knew it. The whole damned court knew it.'

'Not the jury,' said Lyle quietly. He added, 'At least, not the *majority* of the jury.'

They were standing side by side at the pier end, looking out over the broad estuary to where, in the blue distance, the hills and peaks of Wales could be seen against a grey sky. It was possible to feel a touch of warmth in the breeze. Not much, but enough to give promise of one more spring, followed by another summer.

She said, 'Don't make excuses, Mr Lyle. Harry was a fool, in many ways, but he didn't deserve *that*. Ever!'

'Does anybody?'

The following silence was heavy with bitterness and gentle sadness.

Then Lyle said, 'This isn't the end, you know.'

'Mr Justice Littlebright seemed to—'

'Oh, yes.' Lyle's bend of the lips wasn't quite a smile. 'His lordship is as unacquainted with the facts of criminal life as most people.'

'I don't follow.'

'Liz, there never was a gang boss in a wheelchair. Mr Bigs do not officiate from invalid carriages.'

'Oh!'

'And Manser has "got away with it". He's fireproof—in his own opinion. He'll not long take orders from a cripple. He'll oust Taske, if he has to corpse him for the top job.'

'Ah!'

'And,' continued Lyle, 'Manser is no second-edition Taske. He's too wild. He hasn't the cunning. At a guess, he'll shoot his way to the top—and shoot his way into prison. This time, it could easily have been reduced to manslaughter. But murder will come. Nothing surer. And when it does, there'll be some wire-pulling and Littlebright will face Manser across a courtroom again—and this time, Manser will be put away for ever. Judges can make that sort of recommendation. Manser has won a battle, but he'll lose the war.'

'I hope,' sighed Liz.

'Me, too. But, more than that, I *believe.*'